*Don't be la*

Nothing says "Summer's over" quite like the jolt of an alarm clock. I've always believed that all the important things in life happen after 9:00 a.m. so there's no point in getting out of bed before then, but here I am at 7:15 a.m., standing in the shower, getting ready to go somewhere I'm not really that keen on. It's bewildering.

My mom takes transition very seriously, and when I finally make it downstairs after changing my clothes seventeen times, she has the table laid with a crisp blue-gingham tablecloth and matching napkins, fresh-squeezed orange juice, a bowl of cereal, fresh-baked blueberry muffins and yogurt. A little white vase of daisies sits in front of my place. I'm pretty sure that these perky breakfasts aren't going to last. Slowly but surely, the thoughtful little details will vanish as we settle into a routine until it's everyone for herself again. Still, I'm grateful that my mom likes to mark the beginnings of things, and she has not uttered the words, "Is that really what you're wearing?" in about six months …

My mom sits across from me clutching a large coffee mug that says WORLD'S GREATEST MOM. I have no idea where she got it, but I've noticed that she always makes sure the words are facing me when we eat breakfast together …

"This is an important day, honey, first day of eighth grade. I can't believe you're about to start eighth grade! Twenty minutes ago you were four years old!"

"You knew me when I was four?!" I ask in pretend amazement.

"No, but I knew *of* you." She raises an eyebrow …

# Not Fair, Clare

Raincoast Books gratefully acknowledges the financial support of the Province of British Columbia through the BC Arts Council and the Book Publishing Tax Credit and the Government of Canada through the Canada Council for the Arts and the Book Publishing Industry Development Program (BPIDP).

Edited by Elizabeth McLean / Tonya Martin
Cover and interior design by Five Seventeen
Illustrations by Terry Wong

LIBRARY AND ARCHIVES CANADA CATALOGUING IN PUBLICATION

Prinz, Yvonne

    Not fair, Clare / Yvonne Prinz.

ISBN 13: 978-1-55192-984-2
ISBN 10: 1-55192-984-8

    I. Title.

PS8631.R45S74 2008    JC813'.6    C2007-904850-1

Library of Congress Control Number: 2007933943

| Raincoast Books | In the United States: |
| --- | --- |
| 9050 Shaughnessy Street | Publishers Group West |
| Vancouver, British Columbia | 1700 Fourth Street |
| Canada V6P 6E5 | Berkeley, California |
| www.raincoast.com | 94710 |

Raincoast Books is committed to protecting the environment and to the responsible use of natural resources. We are working with suppliers and printers to phase out our use of paper produced from ancient forests. This book is printed with vegetable-based inks on 100% ancient-forest-free, 100% post-consumer recycled, processed chlorine- and acid-free paper. For further information, visit our website at www.raincoast.com/publishing/.

Printed in Canada by Marquis

10  9  8  7  6  5  4  3  2  1

# Not Fair, Clare

BOOK TWO IN
THE CLARE SERIES
BY

Yvonne Prinz

RAINCOAST BOOKS
*Vancouver*

*This book is dedicated to*
*Room To Read — world change starts with educated children.*
*Learn about this organization*
*at www.roomtoread.org*

# Acknowledgements

*Merci*: Alex Green, Lori Katz, Karen Masterson, Linda Coffey, Karen Pearson, Wendel Meldrum, Brandi Shearer, Gail Wadsworth and the Ladies Of The Chorus for continued support; Michelle Benjamin for welcoming me back; Jesse Finkelstein for her patience and sage literary advice; Tonya Martin for her series smarts, Sarah Cooper for watching my back; Elizabeth McLean for endless attention to detail; Dave for not killing me; rebel librarians, booksellers and schoolteachers for working tirelessly to protect our right to read the important books.

# Chapter 1

"My turn." I gently try to pry the binoculars away from Allison, who's been hogging them for the last five minutes.

"One more sec." She peers over the pitch of the roof outside my bedroom window.

I sigh impatiently. "What?"

"A guy. Blond. He's been to the gym. Not my type at all, but then …"

"Let me see." I snatch the binoculars away, forgetting that the strap is around her neck. Allison makes a choking sound as I yank her head toward me.

"Sorry." I untangle the strap from her neck and focus the binoculars on the moving van across the street and then on the young man in question. He's definitely attractive in a sort of sulky "I-hate-everything" way. I pan down his chest as he picks up his end of a plaid sofa. His grey T-shirt says BULLDOG MOVERS. I drop the binoculars and stare at Allison.

"He's the mover."

"He is?" she asks.

"Yeah. They just move the furniture into the house and then they leave. They don't move in."

"I knew that." Allison glares at me. "Where are the artsy, interesting, rebellious but sensitive twin brothers who are to become our boyfriends?"

I peer through the binoculars again as a green Volvo wagon turns in to the driveway. The car barely comes to a stop before the back passenger door flies open. A pale, thin girl wearing a multicoloured clown wig dances over to the movers, yells something at them and then darts over to the front lawn where she completes three cartwheels and a messy backflip faster than a Russian gymnast. The parents stand together in the driveway and clap like parents who have clapped a few too many times.

I groan and hand Allison the binoculars. "Look what we get instead of the twins."

"Yikes," says Allison, focusing. "Those people need to unpack the box with the drugs. That girl needs her medication."

I lie back on the shingles and look up at the sky. Elsa jumps up from inside my bedroom and puts her paws on the windowsill. I lean in and give her smooth, soft head a scratch.

"Look, Elsa, the yappy wiener dog is gone but psycho circus girl has arrived. Allison, what's she doing now?"

"She's walking on her hands. Oops, she just found a little surprise that the wiener dog left behind. She's smelling, she's screaming, she's running and … she's gone." Allison drops the binoculars. "Well, that was fun. So much for the dream." She shifts herself around to face me, lounging against the pitch of the roof with her arms behind her head.

"Can you stay for dinner?" I ask. "My mom's making something Italian."

"Like what?" she asks.

"I don't know, but it ends in 'ini.'"

"Nah, I should go," she says, picking at a fake tattoo of a snake on her arm. "I told my mom and dad I'd eat with them. Mom's been out at the co-op garden all afternoon, and I'm sure she has something yummy with loads of fibre planned for the night before eighth grade starts."

At the words "eighth grade," my heart does a little leap.

"Okay. I'll walk you out." I hoist myself up and push Elsa out of the way so we can crawl back through the window into my bedroom. Elsa follows us down the stairs, tail wagging. I say goodbye to Allison on the front porch and watch her get on her bike and ride slowly past the moving van across the street. At the corner she turns right toward Pine Street and the biosphere, which is what she calls her house. Her dad is an environmental engineer, and he built a house that is almost totally off the grid. Everything in it is either recycled or solar-powered.

Allison's parents are a little more "green" than mine. I'm working on Mom (she still won't recognize tofu as food), but the only "green" my dad appreciates is money. He's a lawyer in the worst possible way. My mom used to be a lawyer, too, but she quit practising when I was twelve because she noticed I was running wild. That's when she decided she wanted to be a "movie-of-the-week" mom, but she's cooled her jets on all that, thank God. Now she's sort of a scary Martha Stewart. She's converted our kitchen into a Betty Crocker test kitchen, which has an obvious upside, but it's tricky getting a plain old peanut-butter-and-jelly sandwich or a bowl of Cap'n Crunch in there. There's a lot of "Taste this," with a big spoon coming at your mouth.

I sit down on the front porch steps with Elsa and watch the movers unload the last bits of furniture into the house across the street. Through the windows I can see the freaky kid running around inside. Elsa's watching, too. Probably looking for a furry playmate; that wiener dog was brutal. The sun is dipping into the horizon and the neighbourhood is bathed in that golden pre-autumn light that makes you miss summer before it's even gone.

I used to hate this time of year. I dreaded the first day of school so much that my stomach would hurt for a week, but everything is different this year. For one thing, I have Allison, my first real best friend ever. We officially met at Track-and-Field camp, but I'd bumped into her in some very strange places before that, like the lingerie department of a department store (don't ask) and then again at a fundraising run for breast cancer. Allison moved into my neighbourhood in the middle of summer vacation. She also moved into my school district, which means she'll be going to my school now.

At first I thought she was way too cool to bother with someone like me, but it turns out that she actually thought the same thing about me, which amazes me. I'm not even sure *I'd* hang out with me if I were her. There are so many things about Allison that make her different from the other kids at school. She always seems to notice the best in people. Like, for instance, if we see someone on the street who's pushing a grocery cart full of empty bottles, she'll say, "Wow, did you see that woman's neck-lace?" Allison will talk to anyone, no matter how weird they are. She's on a first-name basis with the people in my neighbourhood who my mom specifically told me to avoid. And she's not a fashion victim like most of the girls at my school. She loves digging through piles of clothes at thrift stores and Goodwill. She hates makeup and she loves animals. Another cool thing about Allison is that she's really interested in other people's interests. I got her reading comic books and now she's totally hooked, just like me.

Elsa's new, too. A gift from my Aunt Rusty for my birthday in July. I tortured my parents for years, end-lessly begging for a dog, and then Aunt Rusty just shows up with Elsa on my birthday. *Voilà!* Well, that's not the whole truth. She was actually trying to get me to for-give her for stealing my boyfriend. He didn't know he was my boyfriend yet, but I would have told him eventu-ally. His name is Mr. Bianchini and he's my Track coach. Unfortunately, Aunt Rusty and Mr. Bianchini are still an item, which could be awkward now that school is back in. Does a woman stop loving a man just because anoth-er woman has stolen him away? No. She does not. And when Mr. Bianchini comes to his senses, I will, of course, forgive him, too. In the meantime, I have a big furry ball of unconditional love named Elsa, who is off in a blissful puppy coma while I scratch her in all her favourite places.

The other thing that's different about me since last year is that shortly after school let out in June, I got the breasts I'd been praying for (of course no one knew I even cared except Aunt Rusty). I was the last known twelve-year-old in the free world to develop, but at least I don't have to run off and join the circus now. No one's ever going to mistake me for Dolly Parton, but they won't mistake me for a boy either. I have the minimum acceptable chest size for an eighth-grade girl.

The smell of garlic and rosemary floats from the kitchen, through the screen door and up my nose, reminding me that I'm starving. I jump up off the step, Elsa at my heels, and head inside for dinner.

## Chapter 2

Nothing says "Summer's over" quite like the jolt of an alarm clock. I've always believed that all the important things in life happen after 9:00 a.m. so there's really no point in getting out of bed before then, but here I am at 7:15 a.m., standing in the shower, getting ready to go somewhere I'm not really that keen on. It's bewildering.

My mom takes transition very seriously, and when I finally make it downstairs after changing my clothes seventeen times, she has the table laid with a crisp blue-gingham tablecloth and matching napkins, fresh-squeezed orange juice, a bowl of cereal, fresh-baked blueberry muffins and yogurt. A little white vase of daisies sits in front of my place. I'm pretty sure that these perky breakfasts aren't going to last. Slowly but surely, the thoughtful little details will vanish as we settle into a routine until it's everyone for herself again. Still, I'm grateful that my mom likes to mark the beginnings of things, and she has not uttered the words, "Is that really what you're wearing?" in about six months.

At the other end of the table she's stacked my school supplies in a nice neat pile, and I can smell the pink rubber erasers and pencil leads from where I'm sitting. It's weird the way that smell replaces the smell of fresh-cut grass, barbecues and watermelon. It's like the official "fun's-over" smell.

Choosing school supplies with me each year seems to bring my mom a certain satisfaction. I think it's the supply angle that appeals to her. Be prepared for any emergency (always keep puff pastry in the freezer and a can of artichoke hearts in the cupboard in case company shows up unexpectedly). She's oblivious to the fact that these are life-and-death decisions. Let's say you show up with a map-of-the-world pencil case, only to find that the biggest geek in class has exactly the same one. It doesn't bode well for the school year to come. Only the coolest of the cool are allowed to set trends. I carefully scope out what's available and try to stay neutral. No themes, no Barbie, no Mickey Mouse, no Garfield. I learned the hard way that Hello Kitty is a total red flag. I've collected some awesome superhero pencil cases, notebooks and stuff like that, but I'm smart enough to leave them at home.

My mom sits across from me clutching a large coffee mug that says WORLD'S GREATEST MOM. I have no idea where she got it, but I've noticed that she always makes sure the words are facing me when we eat breakfast together. She's wearing sweats, and I know that as soon as I leave the house she'll be off for her daily five-kilometre run. My dad is long gone, up at dawn, coffee and out the door. His coffee cup (no writing on that one) is already upside down in the dishwasher.

Breakfast is really tasty and I tell my mom so. She beams.

"This is an important day, honey, first day of eighth grade. I can't believe you're about to start eighth grade! Twenty minutes ago you were four years old!"

"You knew me when I was four?!" I ask in pretend amazement.

"No, but I knew *of* you." She raises an eyebrow.

I finish breakfast, load up my backpack with stuff until it's heavier than I am, say goodbye to my mom and get on my bike. I've barely gone half a block when I hear someone yelling.

"Hey, wait!"

I look behind me. The odd little girl from across the street is running along beside me on the sidewalk. She is carefully cupping something in her hands. "Hey, I wanna show you something."

I stop my bike and look at her. She's wearing a pajama top and mismatched bottoms, and her feet are bare. Her orangey red hair is almost as wild as yesterday's clown wig. She runs over to the curb, panting, and slowly opens her hands. There's a small frog sitting in her palm next to a chewed piece of pink bubble gum.

"That's a frog!" She beams at me.

"Yes, it is," I say. "Did you catch it?"

She seems not to have heard me. She puts the bubble gum in her mouth and starts chewing furiously. "Do you have a boyfriend?" she asks.

"Who wants to know?" I ask, as though I'm no older than she is.

"I'm Patience," she says, pulling up her pajama top with one hand to expose a shocking white belly with "Patience" written across it in ballpoint pen. Most of the letters are upside down or backwards.

"You're serious? Your name is Patience?" I think this must be some kind of cruel joke her parents are playing on her. Patience doesn't see the irony in her name, I guess, because she seems confused.

"Of course it's my name. I'm not stupid, you know."

"Okay, Patience, I'm Clare. I've gotta go or I'll be late for school."

"Sure, okay. Do you want to play with my dinosaurs later?"

I'm already down the block and I pretend not to hear that. I wave and keep riding. I look back a few seconds later and see her chasing something through the grass. I guess the frog was thinking along the same lines I was — make a run for it. I wonder why Patience doesn't have to go to school today (or perhaps to an institute with bars on the windows).

Moments later I arrive at the school and try to make my way through the crowds to the bike racks where Allison is meeting me. The schoolyard is one big "Here comes everybody." It's amazing what two months can do to a bunch of preteens. You'd think they were putting something in the water. I'm still one of the tallest girls in my grade, but I'm not towering over anyone anymore. The boys have developed long necks and Adam's apples;

the girls have all somehow arrived with department-store makeovers. I get the once-over several times. I can feel their eyes travelling from my unkempt scrawny ponytail, down past my faded Bob Marley T-shirt tucked into my tired jeans, ending at my scuffed loafers without socks. I'm not even a contestant in their fashion beauty pageant, not even worth bothering with.

When I finally spot Allison, I could kiss her. She looks like a scruffier version of me. She's wearing a camouflage tank top, cargo pants and Birkenstocks. Her long brown hair is pulled back with a faded blue bandana, and her signature army-surplus bookbag is slung over her shoulder. I call out to her and she looks relieved to see me. She laughs and looks around, shrugging. I pull my bike up next to hers. She gives my outfit the once-over, too.

"I hope you brought something else to wear for the swimsuit competition," she says.

I point to my backpack. "Naturally. And my tiara's in there, too." We both laugh and I am utterly grateful for the fact that Allison, my new best friend, is standing right next to me, making fun of the kids who never let me quietly be who I am.

I lock our bikes to the bike stand with my lock, and we make our way back through the crowd, catching snippets of conversation. "Her parents caught her in the sauna with …," "He drank so much he …," "She broke up with …," "He's grounded for …" I try to ignore them, but I'm amazed at the stuff I'm hearing. My summer is starting to sound like two months at Camp Sunshine for Prudish Girls compared to theirs.

Once inside we follow the masses down the familiar hallway to the posted class lists of all the homeroom assignments. The lockers lining the hallways have been de-graffitied and the floors descuffed and buffed to a high shine. That should last about twenty minutes. Allison and I have already talked about the fact that it's too much to hope we'll somehow be assigned to the same homeroom. What are the chances? We join the group of eighth graders gathered around the bulletin board, struggling to find their names. I find mine. I'm in 8B. Allison is in 8A. I can't help but notice that Ginny Germain is also in 8A, an idea I hadn't even entertained.

I walk Allison to her new homeroom, which is right next door to mine but a world away. I tell her to play nice with the other kids and I head over to my class. On the way I pass Ginny Germain, who acknowledges me with an unblinking stare. She's talking on a cell phone and is followed by a gaggle of her admirers. I stand in the doorway of 8B and watch as Ginny Germain walks confidently toward classroom 8A and my new best friend.

# Chapter 3

I'm supposed to meet Allison at her locker at 11:45 a.m. My locker, which was assigned to me last week when I registered, is number 26. Easy: my age times two. Allison's locker is number 89, which is easy, too; it's the year she got her dog, Elvis, but backwards. I dump my stuff into my locker, slam it shut and head for Allison's with a purposeful stride, but I see something on the way that stops me in my tracks. Allison is standing in front of her locker, nonchalantly chatting with Ginny Germain! Ginny is smiling and tucking her shiny black hair behind her ears. I smell a rat. This couldn't possibly be a coincidence. If there is an eighth-grade underground mafia, Ginny is most certainly the boss, and I'm betting she pulled the right strings to have her locker next to Allison's. She's always looking for fresh blood.

I rearrange my face into casual and unsuspecting and keep walking. Allison sees me first and smiles her normal sunny smile, but I see Ginny's face darken behind her. I come to a full stop next to Allison and tentatively say "hi." Ginny actually asks me if I've met Allison. Before I can say, "No, you big dope, I'm just standing here for my health," Allison jumps in.

"Clare and I are friends," she says. "We met at track camp."

"Track camp," Ginny says, wrinkling up her nose as though Allison had said Nerd Camp. "How interesting."

"Well, we should get going," I say, trying to herd Allison away from Ginny.

"Oh, hey, Allison," says Ginny as she throws her backpack over her shoulder and checks her face in a mirror on her locker door. "Join us for lunch at our table in the cafeteria." She slams her locker door.

I start to mumble an excuse and Allison says, "Sure," just like that, no consultation, not so much as a glance my way. She doesn't even seem to notice that Ginny is inviting her, not us.

Needless to say, lunch is a humiliating disaster. I end up sitting at the very end of "Ginny's" table, in no man's land. The seating plan was all laid out before we arrived, as if it was a wedding at the Ritz-Carlton dining room or something. Ginny makes sure Allison is sitting next to her and regales her with exciting stories about her summer and all the boys she met at Lake Snothead for Rich Girls. Everyone at the table *oohs* and *aahs* over Ginny's lunch, which is a Japanese bento box filled with tiny morsels of sushi that look more like jewellery than food. She eats with delicate black chopsticks and washes everything down with a chilled bottle of water that was hauled down off the Swiss Alps by virgin goats. My peanut-butter-and-jelly sandwich on sprouted wheat bread looks downright dismal, even though Allison takes a bite of it and pronounces it "Delicious."

I hope for a little time alone with Allison before we head back to class for the afternoon, but Ginny's adventures eat up the entire hour. I can't help but notice that she laughs too long and too loud at all of Allison's jokes, and she keeps touching Allison's arm like they're country-club pals.

Back in my stupid homeroom, I stare out the window, wondering what on Earth happened to my best friend. Was she just hanging around with me till she could latch on to someone better when school started? Maybe she's just getting the lay of the land. Being nice to Ginny could prove to be a good tactic, I suppose. Ginny is at the top of the invitation list for all the parties, and she knows absolutely everyone, but Allison doesn't even care about stuff like that. Or what if she really does? What if she was just pretending not to?

Suddenly I have a horrible thought. Allison knows all my secrets. What if she tells Ginny? What if Allison is actually a secret agent, a trained spy whose mission it is to infiltrate the geek lifestyle and report back to Ginny so they can have big laughs at the next sleepover party? Ugh! I can see it now: Ginny, in her designer pajamas, licking s'mores off her long fingers while Allison tells her about my superhero comic books and my Japanese monster movie obsession and my Spider-Man pajamas and my undying love for Mr. Bianchini, our Track coach!

The buzzer sounds and class is over. It was all a blur; I'm not even sure what the class was. One more class and I can hook up with Allison again and maybe deprogram her.

My last class of the day is Drama. I decided to take it this year because I have to start thinking about my future. An injury could end my running career, so it wouldn't hurt to be an actress, too.

Drama class is held in a small carpeted auditorium at the other end of the school from my homeroom. They built it a year ago after they had about a hundred bake sales to raise money for it. It feels a bit Frankensteined together, like when someone adds a family room onto their house and it doesn't look anything like the rest of the house.

On the way to Drama class, I stop in at the girls' bathroom. Two of Ginny's ladies-in-waiting are in there blotting lipstick and applying eyeshadow. They're chatting away and don't even notice my arrival. From inside the stall, it takes me a minute to realize that they're talking about Allison. One of them is saying how interesting "that new girl" is and how Troy (who's Troy?) has been asking questions about her (questions? School started five seconds ago!). The other girl says that she loves the way she dresses (?), "all super-casual seventies and everything." I can't quite believe what I'm hearing, and I feel like chopped liver as I skulk out of there and head to my class.

I'm a bit late, but it's okay because the teacher's not even there yet. I drop my stuff and sit on the floor with everyone else. It's a pretty small class, your predictable mix of society dropouts, kids who fancy themselves "actors" and the always present handful who thought Drama class sounded easy on the enrolment form. But then I notice this guy who looks a little old for junior high. He's sitting cross-legged on the floor, talking to some kids. I'm not positive, but it looks like he's wearing green operating-room scrubs for pants. Finally he looks over at me and says, "You must be Clare. I'm Eric."

I nod. "How did you know?" I ask.

"You missed roll call, you're the only one unaccounted for. Make yourself comfortable and we'll get started."

I nod again. Wait a second. Last time I checked, the Drama teacher was Ms. Height, a neurotic fortyish woman who constantly looked startled and wore several scarves at once with long flowing skirts, which made her look like a Romanian fortune teller. Who's this guy?

As if in answer to my question, Eric skootches back so that he's facing all of us, still sitting cross-legged on the carpet. He clears his throat and raises his voice. "Okay, I'm brand new here, so if I seem a little lost, feel free to jump in and help me out. My plan for this class is to get us all really comfortable with each other and then work on a few short plays and exercises. The school play this year will be *Macbeth* ..."

Everyone groans.

"Yeah, I know, you'll actually have to crack a book. The actors will mostly be played by ninth graders, and you'll work on costumes, sets, scripts, stuff like that, but if any of you dazzle me with your acting ability, I see no reason why you couldn't make the cut."

Eric is not only new to this school; he's obviously new to teaching. He's got the enthusiasm of a cocker spaniel, but he seems kind of relaxed and comfortable with himself. He has a way of looking each of us right in the eye when he talks, like he's pulling us into his world. He has what my mother would call "an infectious personality." He also looks about nineteen years old, but he's got to be in his twenties.

Eric drops a stack of *Macbeth*s in front of a girl to pass around.

"I'd like you to get going on reading this. I know it's a tough one but don't worry, we'll be reading it in class, too. For Thursday, your assignment is this: I want each of you to go home and think about how you see yourself. Really give it some thought. We're all individuals with our own memories; we each have a unique identity. After you think about it for a while, I want you to collect anything, like photos, pictures from magazines, words, bits of clothing, anything at all that you feel represents who you are and what you're about. For today, I've got big pieces of cardboard stacked up in the back of the class. Partner up and take turns tracing each other's bodies on them and then cut out the outlines of yourselves. On Thursday we'll glue the stuff you gather in the next couple of days onto these, and then each of you will get some time to share your interpretations of 'You' with the class. Everyone got it?"

Nobody says anything. They're already busy looking around for partners. I'm a little slow on the draw, and then I realize that the class has an odd number of people. I'm left without a partner.

Eric looks over at me kindly. "Clare, you can be my partner, okay?"

"Sure," I say, wanting to kiss him for obliterating a potentially awkward situation.

I lie down on the cardboard, looking up at Eric. He grabs a Magic Marker and looks at me while he addresses the class. "You can do anything you want with your arms and legs. Be creative."

I make a peace sign with my left hand, and Eric kneels down and starts tracing me with the marker. He leaves a good bit of space around my body for a border, which, for obvious reasons, I'm grateful for. Still, it's weird and I try not to look at his eyes, which is sort of impossible. The thing that I notice the most about his face is that it's filled with kindness; it's as though he has the eyes of a sweet old man in the body of a boy. He has freckles around his nose and tiny lines around his eyes.

When he finishes, I stand up and he hands me the marker. He grabs another piece of cardboard and drops it on the floor and lies down on top of it. I wasn't quite prepared for this, but he seems unfazed, so I kneel down next to him, concentrating hard on tracing his outline. I start at his head and he has to pull his tangled reddish blond hair out of the way so I don't write on it. He tucks it behind his head, and the marker squeaks its way down to his feet. I leave the same border on his outline that he did on mine. When I get back up to his head, he smiles at me and jumps up to look at the outline like a ten-year-old would.

"Wow, is my head really that fat?" he laughs.

"No. I was trying not to write on your hair," I say. "You can make it smaller when you cut it out."

"Good tip," he says.

The rest of the class is laughing at their crime-scene outlines, already more relaxed with each other. Eric points to a bucket of scissors at the back of the room and tells us to start cutting them out. I sit on the floor and get to work. I'm grateful for the distraction. I haven't thought about the Allison crisis for almost an hour.

# Chapter 4

After school I meet Allison back at the bike stands. She doesn't look the least bit sheepish; in fact, she looks really happy to see me.

"So, how's your homeroom?" I ask.

"Great!" she says. "Everyone's been so nice to me. I know I'm the new kid and all, but it's been a breeze so far."

"Super!" I say in the same extra-cheerful voice she's using. I bend over and unlock our bikes.

"What's your homeroom like?" she asks.

"Prisonlike," I say, pulling my bike out of the stand and hoisting my backpack onto my shoulders.

"Well, it's only the first day. Don't you think you should give it a little time?" Allison gets on her bike and we start pedalling away from the schoolyard side by side.

"Nope. I pretty much know I hate it."

"Hey, Chuckles," she says. "Save some laughs for the ride home, okay?"

I ignore that. "What would you know about it, anyway?" I say. "You're the 'New Girl.'" I let go of my handlebars to make quotation signs with my fingers.

"Am I supposed to apologize for that or something?" she says, looking indignant.

"No, I just think you should be careful. The sharks are circling, if you know what I mean."

"Could you speak English, please? What is that supposed to mean?"

"Nothing. But Ginny Germain can be a little two-faced. Be careful what you tell her."

"Geez, Clare, give me some credit. I've got a decent set of Spidey-Senses, too, you know. Besides, she doesn't seem so awful to me. You shouldn't worry so much."

But I am worried. Allison and Ginny will be together five days a week for the whole school year. Same homeroom, lockers next to each other. I'm afraid to ask if their desks are close. Location is everything in junior-high society. Harping on about Ginny right now will make me look petty and insecure, though, so I change the subject.

"Hey, have you met the new Drama teacher?"

"They're all new to me," she says, veering off to the left and into the parking lot of the Dairy Delite. She looks over her right shoulder at me.

"After-school snack, anyone?" she asks, grinning.

I follow her into the parking lot and stay outside with the bikes while she runs in and gets two chocolate-dipped cones. We lean against the window ledge, licking our cones.

"So, you were saying about the new Drama teacher," says Allison.

"Well, he's just … unusual," I say, catching a slippery chunk of chocolate with my mouth before it escapes.

"Meaning?"

"I don't know, inspiring, I guess. He's making us read *Macbeth*, but I'm sort of looking forward to it."

"Wow, that *is* inspiring. I'll tell you who's not inspiring is my Shop teacher, Mr. McRonskey. I almost nodded off during the safety portion of the lecture."

"They call him Mr. Mc-Yawn-ski. Didn't you know that?"

"No. How would I know that? But I can see why. His students are likely to get so bored they'll doze off and saw a hand clean off or something. I'm surprised it hasn't happened yet. Did I mention that I'm the only girl in the class? Don't any other girls want to learn how to make a birdhouse?"

I look at her skeptically. "You know you're not there because of the birdhouse."

"Okay, I admit it, I'm making a feminist statement. There's no reason why women shouldn't learn to operate power tools. How come I'm the only girl who wants to make a feminist statement?"

"You'd have a hard time finding an eighth-grade girl at our school who even knows what a feminist is," I say, sculpting my ice cream with my tongue.

"I think you're probably right."

"Mr. Mc-Yawn-ski is the price you have to pay for your statement."

"Maybe I'll transfer over to Art class. Art can be a statement, too. I wonder if it's too late."

"Don't be too hasty. The Art teacher is about a thousand years old, and she makes her students draw the same apple every day for months at a time."

"Good to know."

We lick our ice cream down to the cone. I eat my cone, but Allison tosses hers away. She hates the cone part. We hop back on our bikes. Just before we ride off in separate directions, I ask Allison what she has planned for the weekend. Which actually means, "What are we doing this weekend?"

"Ginny Germain invited me to a party Saturday night. It's at some guy named Troy's house. You want to come?"

"You're going?" I ask, shocked.

"I don't know. I thought I might. If my mom lets me."

"I'd rather stick needles in my eyes," I say.

"You're kidding, right?" she says.

"No. Besides, she invited you. She didn't invite me."

"I'm inviting you."

I look at her, bewildered. How can she not see Ginny's agenda?

"Well, I'll call you. We'll talk about it, okay?"

"Sure," I say. I can already feel the prickle of tears behind my eyes.

Allison pedals away. I watch her brown ponytail bob behind her. I get back on my bike and head toward my street. I'm not quite sure how this happened. One minute we're best friends and the next she's partying with Ginny Germain! Did I black out and miss the chapter where Allison pulls her face off and reveals her alien self?

Tears start to slide over my cheeks as I speed up my tree-lined street. This is all starting to feel very familiar.

Suddenly I hear someone calling my name. I slow down and look around. It's got to be Allison. It was all a trick she was playing on me. We'll laugh about this one forever.

But it's not Allison. It's that wretched little girl from across the street. She's standing in the exact same spot where I left her this morning. She's chewing gum furiously.

"Hi! What are you, deaf or something? Didn't you hear me calling you? Remember when you said you would play with my dinosaurs?"

"How do you know my name?" I ask, quickly wiping my face on my sleeve.

"You told me this morning."

"Oh, right." I groan.

"Your mom gave me a cookie."

I notice that she's wearing most of the cookie on her face, her T-shirt and her hands.

"I'm pretty busy right now," I say, trying to execute a hasty retreat and making a mental note to come home through the alley from now on.

"Do you know how to kiss a boy?" she asks, twisting her T-shirt into a knot with one hand and scratching a mosquito bite on her cheek with the other.

"Why?" I ask, astonished.

"Well, your mom says you're thirteen, and that's the year you start to kiss boys. So do you?"

"Of course I do," I lie. This is great. I now have a psychotic little canary to remind me of my lack of experience with boys, as though it weren't bad enough already.

"Show me," she says.

"Show you? Are you kidding?" I start to pedal away. "I've gotta go now."

When I look back, Patience is standing on the sidewalk, apparently unaware that I've left. She seems to be kissing the top of her hand with her chocolate-chip lips. Suddenly she looks over her shoulder at me, her eyes locking onto me like a bird of prey's.

"My mom says you can babysit me if you're really thirteen!" she yells after me.

When I don't respond, she yells louder, "We have cable!"

# Chapter 5

I let myself in the front door and wander into the kitchen. I drop my backpack on the kitchen table next to a plate of chocolate-chip cookies and a note:

*Clare,*

*Hi honey, I hope school was great today. I'm at the shelter. Have some cookies. Elsa's in the backyard. I'll be home by five.*

*Love you,*
*Mom*

A likely story. She was probably trying to ditch Patience, just like me. But my mom does volunteer at a women's shelter. She gives free legal advice. She started volunteering a couple of months ago when she donated all her old power suits to the shelter because she finally figured out that she wasn't ever going to wear them again. I explained to her that you can't really wear Armani to a PTA meeting when you're on the Cookie Committee; it scares the other moms. I also vetoed the briefcase she kept carrying after I snapped it open one day and found an apple and a lipstick. Now she carries a big slouchy leather bag that can fit dinner for four if you need it to.

I make my way to the back door to let Elsa in, stopping at the answering machine, which is blinking, to hit play:

"Hey, it's Rusty. Clare, you've gotta call me. I need a date for this poetry slam on Saturday night. One of my friends is reading. You're totally gonna love it. Call me, call me, call me, 'kay? Bye."

A poetry slam? I don't even know what that is. And why can't Mr. Bianchini go with her? Hmmm, maybe there's trouble in paradise.

I open the back door and call Elsa. Normally she would have heard me come in and been barking at the door, but she's not there. I call her a couple more times, but she doesn't come. I walk out onto the deck and look around. I can't see her anywhere. I start calling her again, louder this time. I run to the end of the yard and follow the fence around to the front gate. She's nowhere. I check the gate. It's closed. I'm fighting the panic I'm starting to feel, but my heart is already in my throat and my mouth is dry. Elsa has never left the yard without me, she doesn't know about traffic, and what if someone stole her? She's so friendly she'd go with anyone. Finally I see something. Along the fence that faces the back alley, there's a hole in the dirt. Elsa loves to dig. The hole is definitely big enough for her to squeeze under the fence.

I open the back gate and start running down the alley, calling her. Every time I see a person, I stop and describe

Elsa to them. No one has seen her. I keep running, calling her, praying she's okay. I promise to be a better person if she's okay. I promise to play dinosaurs with Patience if she's okay. I go up one street and down another, then double back and do the alleys. I keep going for forty-five minutes. I stop to catch my breath for a second, but then I start running again. My feet are getting heavy and I'm getting a sinking feeling. I start making a plan in my head. I'll find Elsa's best photo, make posters, organize a search party. Call the pound, the SPCA. I can't believe I've lost Elsa. How could this be happening today of all days?

I head down into a ravine, crashing through the bushes, calling Elsa every few steps. On the other side of the ravine I come out into a park. I scan the horizon and then run across the ball fields to the far side of the park. I see someone sitting on a bench in the shade. As I get closer I see that the person is a girl. She's wearing a long dress with little lavender flowers on it, and she's petting a dog. She appears to be talking to it. The dog is listening to her with ears cocked. The dog is Elsa. I run toward her, calling. She turns to look at me and so does the person who's talking to her.

"Elsa?" I stand there stunned.

"What did you expect? You've been screaming my name all over the neighbourhood like a maniac. Couldn't you just send me a note like in the old days?" She scratches Elsa's head. "Nice dog. What's her name?"

I hesitate a second, then blurt it out. "Elsa."

"What?" she says impatiently.

"No. My dog's name. It's Elsa."

Suddenly it all clicks for her. "You named your dog after *me*!" she screams. "Do I remind you of a dog? Is that it?"

"No, it's just that we sort of went our separate ways and I wanted something to remember you by."

Elsa's face softens and she looks at my dog. "Well, she does have my hair colour, and she's awfully cute."

I sit down next to Elsa on the park bench and catch my breath. Elsa the dog jumps up on me and licks my face. "You're grounded," I say and bury my face in her fur. I'm perplexed that she seems to be able to see Elsa the person. How is that possible? I invented Elsa out of thin air when I was four. I thought I was the only one who could see her.

"You realize that this is going to get very confusing," says Elsa. "You should probably change her name to something more doggish, like Spot or Fluffy or Sport or something. How about Champ? Champ is good."

"I can't," I say. "She's already trained to respond to Elsa."

Elsa looks at me with her classic "You've-got-to-be-kidding" look. "You've been running around for the better part of an hour, screeching her name, and this dog has been sitting right here ignoring you. How is that responding, exactly?"

"Okay, okay. Maybe we could come up with something close like … um. I know! How about Elsie?"

Elsa shrugs. "She's your dog."

"Okay, now I have to retrain everybody else, too."

Elsa sighs. "I'm really flattered that you cared enough about me to name this hairy, misbehaved, slightly smelly creature after me, but you should have given the whole idea a little more thought. Did you really think that you would never, ever need me again? That's a bit optimistic, don't you think?"

"All right. Bad idea." I pick up a twig and tap Elsie on each side of her doggy shoulders. "I dub thee 'Elsie,' woman's best friend and all-around fun dog." Elsie grabs the twig and plays tug-of-war with me till it breaks.

Elsa rolls her eyes.

I slouch down on the bench with my hand on Elsie's head and sigh mournfully.

"Okay," says Elsa, "let's get down to business. Tell me everything and don't leave anything out."

I tell her all about Allison, Ginny Germain, the cafeteria disaster, the party, the lockers, the homeroom, Drama class. Elsa listens thoughtfully, never once interrupting, nodding here and there, grimacing, biting her lip. When I'm finished, I feel relieved to have shared it all with someone. I wait for some reassurance, but she's not saying anything.

"Elsa?" I say.

"I'm thinking."

"Oh." I sit patiently.

"Okay." She sits up straight and faces me. "Here's my take on this. You're going to have to pull back. Let the

Ginny thing run its course. You and I know who Ginny is, but Allison is going to have to find out for herself. Allison is a good person and she'll come around on her own. I guarantee it."

"But what do I do in the meantime? Without Allison I'm back to being Clare the Geek."

"I'll tell you what you do." She rearranges herself on the bench.

"What?" I ask impatiently.

"You become the youngest girl ever to play Lady Macbeth."

"Lady Macbeth! Are you crazy? Do you have any idea how hard that play is?"

"Of course. That's why it's perfect for you."

I think about this and I slowly start to smile.

"*Your noble friends do lack you*," says Elsa, raising her chin.

"What does that mean?" I ask.

"Read the play and find out."

"I don't know, Elsa. It's a really long play. Lady Macbeth has a million lines and I'm only an eighth grader."

"Okay, well, maybe they'll let you sell Kool-Aid and cookies at intermission. Is that more your speed?"

I think about it a moment. "Okay, I'll do it. But then what?"

"Well, it's a two-part plan. While you're busy becoming Lady Macbeth, you won't have time to worry about what's going on with Allison and Ginny. Allison, meanwhile, will come to see Ginny for the power-hungry narcissist that she is and be back just in time to celebrate your acting debut."

"Sounds great, but what if I don't get the part?"

"I won't entertain such negative thoughts. Take that unruly beast home and start learning your lines."

I wander back home, with Elsie wagging her tail at my side. The sun is still warm on the back of my neck and I take my time getting home so I can mull over what Elsa just told me. I wonder if I'm strong enough to let Allison figure out what kind of person Ginny is. Do I have enough faith in our friendship to wait this out? I'm not so sure.

I explain to my mom and dad that Elsa has now become Elsie, which leaves them both looking a little befuddled. I don't expect them to understand.

After dinner I start on *Macbeth*. At first Shakespeare's words are awkward in my mouth and hard to understand, but eventually I can see why Elsa would suggest that I audition for the part. Lady Macbeth is deliciously evil and ambitious; she is sly and artful as she coaxes her husband into killing Duncan, the king. I pace around my bedroom, book in hand, delivering Lady Macbeth's lines to Elsie, who couldn't be less interested. Before long I'm really starting to enjoy the language of *Macbeth*. Reciting the lines makes me feel like a different person. To make it seem more real, I pull an inside-out T-shirt over my head for a veil and wrap my bedsheet around me.

"... *when in swinish sleep*
*Their drenched natures lie as in a death,*
*What cannot you and I perform upon*
*The unguarded Duncan? What not put upon*
*His spongy officers, who shall bear the guilt*
*Of our great quell?*"

Things are about to get pretty bloody around the castle.

# Chapter 6

It's my turn to go up to the front of the Drama class with my cardboard self and tell everyone about who I am. I sit on the stool and bend my cardboard cutout at the knees and the top of the thighs so it can sit on my lap like a ventriloquist's dummy. I clear my throat and start at my head.

"These are my favourite superheros, Spider-Man and the Green Lantern." I move down to my neck. "Here's a picture of my dog, Elsie." Over to my left arm. "These are the ribbons I've won at track meets. This one is from the district final; I placed second in the eight-hundred metres." Right arm. "These are some people I sort of admire. That's John Lennon, this is Roy Lichtenstein, that's Jacques Cousteau. This is Ridley Scott. He ... um ... directed *Blade Runner*, my favourite movie. Over here is a picture of a scene from that movie."

Eric is watching me as though I've just discovered a cure for cancer. But I've noticed that he seems to be that excited about everyone's cutout.

"What do the heads represent, Clare?" He points to the Barbie doll heads that I've stapled to my cardboard stomach.

"Well, I have a collection of them. I'm not sure they represent anything."

"Just the heads?" he says, grinning.

"Yeah." I make a point of not smiling back.

I continue down to the fingers on my right hand. "These are ticket stubs from all the movies I went to last summer, mostly Japanese monster movies and anime. I have a lot because I saw a few of them more than once." I point to a black-and-white photo-booth picture next to the ticket stubs. "This is me with my friend Paul. I put him here because he and I used to like all the same stuff. I mean, he probably still does, but he had to go away to a private school. I drew in his dad because I didn't have a photo," I say, pointing to a drawing of a monster with large teeth and horns, holding a gun. "He's the guy who sent Paul away." I point to my left leg and a photo of Aunt Rusty that my mom took at her gallery opening. "This is my Aunt Rusty," I say. "She's kind of weird but kind of cool, too. She's standing in front of one of her paintings."

Eric points to another photo. "What's that photo of?" he asks.

"Oh, that's the view from the rooftop of my house, outside my bedroom window. I spend a lot of time there."

Eric nods. "Who's that?" he says, pointing to a drawing that takes up my entire right thigh. It's coloured in with pastel crayons.

"That's a good friend of mine."

"Is that a beret she's wearing?"

"Yes," I say. "She lives in Paris."

"I see," says Eric. "Well, Clare, that was outstanding. Let's give Clare a hand, everyone."

Everyone claps the way junior-high kids are expected to clap, without any enthusiasm, but I can tell by the way their eyes follow me back to my seat that they think I'm more interesting today than I was on Monday. Unfortunately, interesting only matters in Drama class.

My cutout and I sit down on the carpet next to my books. I try to pay attention to the other kids in class as they, one by one, sit on the stool with their cutouts and describe themselves to the rest of us. I'm having trouble concentrating because I'm obsessed with two things. One of them is Allison. She didn't call last night, and I didn't meet her in our spot this morning. I came late and got to my homeroom just as the hallways were emptying. The other one is Lady Macbeth. I stayed up late reading *Macbeth* and now I'm convinced that Elsa was right about trying out for the part. I figure I'll stay after class and talk to Eric about it. I know it's a long shot, but I already have some of the lines memorized, and maybe if he knows I'm serious about it he'll encourage me and even help me. The end-of-class buzzer rings and I take my time collecting my things until all the other kids are gone. Eric is tidying up for his next class. I walk over to him.

"Um, Eric? Can I ask you something?"

"Sure, Clare, what's up?" He stops what he's doing and leans against the desk he never sits at, crosses his arms and looks directly into my eyes.

"Well, the thing is, I've been reading *Macbeth* and I was wondering if you would let me read for the part of Lady Macbeth?"

Eric looks surprised. "That's a really big part. Are you sure you're ready to tackle something like that?"

"Yeah, I'm positive," I say, feeling bolder by the minute. Something about Eric's kind blue eyes makes me feel very brave.

"Plus, if you got the part, there would be tons of rehearsals, after school, weekends, that kind of thing. Can you make a commitment like that?"

"Yes. I'm not married, I don't have any children and I'm currently unemployed," I say.

Eric grins. "Ah, so you're a drifter." His eyes narrow. "How do I know I can trust you?"

"You don't. You'll just have to take my word for it." I say.

Eric's face changes: "*I have done the deed. Didst thou not hear a noise?*"

I reply, "*I heard the owl scream and the crickets cry.*"

"Good," says Eric. "I was just checking. Keep working on your lines. You'll get a fair shake. Remember to study Lady Macbeth's character. Learn about *who* she is, not just what she says. That's what's going to get you the part, okay?"

"Okay." I smile at him as I grab my pack and dash out the door, dodging the kids filing in for the next class.

In eighth grade you're allowed two optional classes. I'm taking Drama and Track and Field. Optional classes fall either two or three times a week, depending on what week it is. A person needs a degree in physics, a calendar, a calculator and a protractor to figure out the system. I do know that my next class is Track and Field with Mr. Bianchini. I also know that Allison is in that class and so is Ginny Germain and I am, once again, late.

By the time I get my shorts on and get out to the field, Mr. Bianchini is already doing his "Welcome-to-Track-and-Field" speech. I sit on the grass at the back, a few rows behind Allison and Ginny. Allison seems to be looking around for someone and I'm pretty sure it's me, but I stay out of sight. I watch Allison's brown ponytail bob up and down as she nods in agreement with whatever Mr. Bianchini is saying. Next to her, Ginny's sleek black hair is held back by something very familiar. At first I can't place it. Then I realize it's Allison's faded blue bandana.

A lump rises in my throat. I hug my knees and try to listen to Mr. Bianchini. I used to hang on every word he said, but now it's as if I've heard it all before. Also, I'm wondering why I've never noticed that he sounds an awful lot like Elmer Fudd. How can Aunt Rusty stand it?

We stand up, eventually, to run the 1,500 metres. Allison finally spots me and strides directly over to me.

"Hey, where were you this morning? I waited forever. I thought you were sick or something."

Ginny glowers at me from behind her.

"Nope," I say. "I just decided to leave a little later."

Allison looks confused. "Whaddya mean, a little later?"

I shrug as I head over to the track and start jogging. Allison falls in next to me with Ginny close behind.

"Okay, what's going on?" Allison asks, looking hurt.

Ginny catches up and jogs next to Allison. "Leave her alone, Allison. Clare's a loner. She always has been. Right, Clare?"

Allison ignores Ginny, but I glare at her. "You don't know the first thing about me," I say. I stop running so that the entire class passes me. I bend over and pretend to tie my shoelace. Allison looks over her shoulder at me as she runs along next to Ginny. I stand up and watch Allison getting smaller. I want to cry. Mr. Bianchini yells to me from the sidelines, asking if I'm okay. I nod and start running slowly around the track.

## Chapter 7

Dear Elsa,

I know you're out there somewhere. As for me, I'm hiding out on the roof. Patience spotted me this morning. She's like a heat-seeking missile. I was just grabbing the newspaper and she was all over me. She wanted me to look at her scar. I get the feeling that she has a never-ending supply of things to show me. She said she fell through a glass window when she was four because she saw it on TV. (Saw what on TV? A man telling her to jump through the window? What channel is she watching?) I pretended to be so grossed out by the scar on her wrist that I had to go inside. The truth is, it was pretty nasty. Part of me feels a bit sad for her, she's such a strange kid. Another part of me fears her.

Operation Lady Macbeth has been launched. I'm learning the lines, I'm living the part, I'm loving the part. I must have the part.

The funny thing is that the more I learn about Lady Macbeth, the more I understand Ginny Germain. Lady Macbeth will stop at nothing to be queen; she'll manipulate, lie and even kill. She's ruthless. Okay, maybe Ginny wouldn't have someone kill me to get to my best friend, but I bet she would if she lived a few centuries ago. I'm pretty sure that Allison is at a party with Ginny right now at someone named Troy's house. I'm trying desperately not to think about it but it's tearing me apart. Aunt Rusty is taking me to a poetry slam tonight. I don't even know what that is, but it's better than hanging around here. My mom and dad are renting a movie. I heard my mom yell at my dad to bring home something "romantic" as he headed out to the video store, and there was talk of popcorn.

I'm outta here.

Not Fair,

Clare

Aunt Rusty and I are sitting on hard wooden chairs at a tiny round table. We're at the coffee house where the poetry slam is being held. I think it's weird that a place like this is called a coffee house, since coffee seems to be the last thing on anyone's mind. It's more of a bizarre art gallery where unusual people in strange clothes come to post their flyers about drumming circles and massage. In fact, one entire wall is plastered with a patchwork of multicoloured flyers that flap in the breeze every time someone opens the door.

I'm noticing that no one is wearing padding of any sort and no one looks armed or especially dangerous, so I'm thinking that the "slam" part of poetry slam is just a figure of speech. Aunt Rusty has assured me that no one gets hurt at these things. Even so, I'm not at all comfortable, and I peek over the rim of my decaf caffe latte at the assortment of eccentrics surrounding me. There's the usual tattoos and piercings and shaved heads that I've come to associate with Aunt Rusty's crowd, but there are a few people here who make her crowd look positively tame. For instance, a bald man a few tables to my left is wearing a large snake as a necktie. I try not to stare. This is the kind of place where you're a little bit afraid to use the ladies' room.

Aunt Rusty and I are catching up. I used to see a lot more of her before she started dating my Track coach. For some reason, though, I can no longer remember what all the fuss was about. Is it possible that I've fallen out of love with Mr. Bianchini? Does it happen that easily? Come to think of it, I haven't thought about Mr. Bianchini once since this whole Allison thing started. In fact, when I look at Aunt Rusty, who tonight has chosen to wear black leather pants and a T-shirt that says SHUT UP on it, it's hard to picture the two of them as a couple.

Aunt Rusty is telling me about the paintings she's been working on.

"Yeah," she says, putting her coffee cup down. Her bright red lipstick stains the rim. "I'm working with different colours now, lighter colours, like yellow. Yellow is a remarkable colour. I spent all of yesterday and the day before exploring yellow."

"What about white?" I ask.

"I'm not ready for white yet," she says decisively. "Maybe this winter."

Aunt Rusty asks me about school, and I fill her in on all the stuff that's been going on. I've always loved Aunt Rusty's viewpoint and I've trusted her with lots of secrets.

"Ginny. She's the one we hate, right?"

"Right," I say.

Aunt Rusty takes a sip of her coffee. "Allison's cool. She's just going through 'New-Girl' syndrome. It passes when the next new girl arrives. You see, there can only be one new girl at a time."

This makes sense to me. I watch out of the corner of my eye as an old woman wearing a long black dress and black boots goes from table to table asking if anyone would like their fortune told.

"So you're auditioning for Lady Macbeth?" Aunt Rusty says. "She's my absolute favourite Shakespearean character. I painted her once, you know."

"You did? How did you know what she looks like?" I ask.

"What do you think she looks like?"

I shrug.

"Exactly. It's open to interpretation."

The fortune teller is suddenly at our table. Aunt Rusty asks her how much she charges. The woman tells her five dollars, Aunt Rusty pulls out a chair and the woman sits down with us. Aunt Rusty points to me and the woman places a deck of cards in front of me. She tells me to separate the deck into three piles. I do. Then she tells me to take the top card off each pile and turn it over. She looks long and hard at my face, which creeps me out. She smells like patchouli.

"You are troubled," she says. "So young, yet so troubled."

She looks down at the cards. "This first card, a celebration. There is a party somewhere?"

I nod.

"This next card is jealousy." She touches it with a red fingernail. "Something unsettling is going to happen at this party. The third card is very, very important. It's the rival card. Your rival is at this party and an incident will cause her to be jealous. Do you understand?"

I don't but I nod anyway. I had no idea that fortune tellers could be so specific. Aunt Rusty nods with me, but she looks more amused than anything.

The woman tells me to pick three more cards. I choose "Good News," "Hope," and "Misunderstanding." She tells me that I will hear some good news about something I have been hoping for (duh). Then she tells me there's been a misunderstanding and I am partly to blame. She tells me to pick one final card off any pile. I choose "Death." Suddenly her smile fades and she looks pale. She shakes her head and her giant gold earrings jingle.

"Little girl, have you been thinking about death?" she says, almost accusingly.

I look down at the dancing skeleton on the card.

"No," I say. "Oh, wait, yes, I've been studying Lady Macbeth."

The woman appears relieved. "Thank God!" She looks toward the heavens, or in this case the pipes crisscrossing the ceiling. She picks up the death card and spits on it three times. "Ptuh! Ptuh! Ptuh!" She puts it back in the deck and her smile returns. Aunt Rusty loses it and lets out an audible snort. I glare at her.

"It's not so bad," the fortune teller says, gathering up the cards and dropping them into a silk patchwork bag. "Mostly good, really. What's broken shall be fixed." She places her gnarled hand on mine. "Don't think so much, huh?"

She holds an open palm toward Aunt Rusty, who digs a crumpled five-dollar bill out of her bag and gives it to her.

The woman leaves just as a guy in a beret turns the microphone on and gets the poetry slam rolling.

The rules are simple. Poets are allowed three minutes onstage. Chosen members of the audience are the judges. A poet can get up to ten points for a poem. The general audience is allowed to react any way it sees fit.

The first poet is the guy with the snake. His poem is called "Dancing with Chloe." I think Chloe is the snake because he seems to be talking to her. The audience tires of this quickly and starts booing and hissing like snakes until he skulks off the stage. I don't boo or hiss myself. I think you should be careful how you treat a man holding a large snake.

The next poet is Aunt Rusty's friend, Alex. Aunt Rusty cheers for him when he gets onstage and he waves at her self-consciously. He looks about twenty-five and is wearing a pilly green sweater and plaid pants. His hair is black and it looks as though he's been driving with his head out the window for a while. He starts right in on his poem. Apparently no one wants to waste any of the three minutes. Alex's voice is clear and melodic. The audience becomes quiet and strains to catch every word:

"*Probably Miles*

*And the girl on the bicycle gave the café boy a flower*
*with a small piece of paper around the stem.*
*And I still don't know much about flowers,*
*but it looked blue and drooping as if to say,*
*That's me sometimes when you're not looking.*

*And when she sped past me*
*I wanted to grab the front wheel,*
*feel the rubber blurry in my palm,*
*let smoke travel up my wrist and say,*
*I am probably for you.*

*But my hands were slow even then;*
*the pavement cracked,*
*the city continued,*
*and it just kept getting worse.*"

The audience cheers. Aunt Rusty whoops. Alex shuffles to his chair in the back. I'm not sure what the poem means, but I think I was moved by the way he recited it. If I had read it in a book, I might not have been excited about it, but here in the coffee house it sounds like the best poem ever written.

The poets continue to spill their guts on the stage. Aunt Rusty was right. No one gets physically hurt, but egos are stomped on. The audience is vicious.

After listening to ten more poets, some good, some great, some awful, the judges get together to add up their scores, and the guy in the beret announces that Alex has won. Aunt Rusty whoops again. Alex comes back on the stage and walks off with a cool fifty bucks. Aunt Rusty asks him to join us for a coffee. He sits quietly, drinking peppermint tea out of a large cup and saucer. Aunt Rusty's comfortable doing most of the talking. They talk about music and art and artists and friends they have in common.

I watch Alex's long thin fingers fold an empty packet of sugar into halves until it's tiny, a habit we share. I finally work up the nerve to tell him that I loved his poem, and he grins at me and says, "Yeah, really?" I nod and blush furiously. He doesn't seem to notice. I love it when people don't feel like they have to point out the fact that you're blushing. Anyone who is blushing knows it already. When Alex gets up to leave, he digs a book out of his backpack and gives it to me. It's not so much a book as a bunch of pages stapled at the spine to make it look like a book.

"Here. This is a free copy of my poems. I give it to all my fans."

"Thanks," I say. "That's really nice of you."

He shrugs. "There's plenty more where that came from. I've only got about seven fans."

I look at the cover of the book. It's a picture of a store window filled with doll parts — plastic heads, legs and arms. Underneath it is the title of the book: *Limited Parts and Service*. I look up as Alex walks out the door and into the night.

Aunt Rusty always tells me that if you're unhappy, you should step out of your life for a while. And somehow, sitting here with Aunt Rusty in this strange place, away from my life, I can almost imagine everything being okay.

# Chapter 8

> *"But screw your courage to the sticking place."*
> LADY MACBETH

On Monday my world starts to change in mysterious ways. The weird thing is that I don't know if it's coming unravelled or improving dramatically. I feel as though I'm watching a tiny bit of water trickle through a stone wall, knowing that at any time the wall will collapse and a river of water will explode over it and nothing will be the same.

I walk to school. One reason I do this is that without the bike I can hide behind bushes quickly if I see Patience approaching. The other reason is that I'm sporting a look I think is more appropriate for aspiring actors. Black turtleneck, black hairband, black heavy-soled boots. Picture this look on a bike. It just doesn't work. I know it practically killed my mom, but she never said a word.

When I arrive at school, the hallways are buzzing with post-party gossip. Being a fringe dweller, I can only gather snippets of information and try to put the story together like a puzzle. It seems that Troy (who *is* this guy?) is interested in Allison, which would be great for Allison and Troy (whoever he is) except that Ginny sort of has a thing for Troy, which makes it complicated. Ginny has always had her pick of the boys. Not only the boys from our school but the boys from every school, soccer team, football team, softball team and track team in the area. As far as I know, no boy has ever chosen another girl over Ginny. Suddenly Ginny is getting competition from a rookie she hand-picked as one of her loyal subjects. The weirdest part is that the fortune teller was right — or just very lucky.

I have a new mantra: what would Lady Macbeth do? I think of Ginny as a modern-day Lady Macbeth, manipulating people, twisting the truth. If I watch Ginny closely, I can pick up tips on how to play Lady Macbeth. I wonder if Allison knows what she's in for. I wish I could warn her, but we've been avoiding each other. I try to remember what Elsa told me. *Wait until this Ginny thing plays out.* It's probably good advice, but I miss Allison almost all the time.

I pass the day in a fog. Math (who cares?), Science (yawn), Social Studies (puhleese!). At lunch I take my egg salad sandwich out to a quiet corner in the schoolyard and practise my Lady Macbeth lines between bites, telling myself over and over, "It's not what you say, it's how you say it."

Finally it's time for Drama class. I try to look brooding and disinterested as I drop my pack on the carpet and sit down next to it. In reality my heart is leaping with excitement. Eric is talking to a boy on the other side of the room.

He gives the guy a friendly punch in the shoulder and stands up. "Welcome. I hope everyone had a great weekend and I know you all took some time to start working your way through *Macbeth*."

The class looks sheepish and avoids Eric's eyes. Eric is undaunted.

"Okay, did anyone in class take some time to read *Macbeth*, anyone at all?"

I slowly raise my hand.

"Aha, Clare. Great." He gives my new look an approving once-over but doesn't say anything. "Come on up here."

My hands start to shake as I grab my book and walk to the front of the class. I can feel prickling in my armpits and I'm starting to think the black turtleneck wasn't such a great idea.

"Okay," says Eric, "how about we start with Act One, Scene Five. Lady Macbeth is reading a letter from her husband. He's telling her what he's heard from the three witches. Duncan, the king, is on his way to the castle, and Lady Macbeth plots his murder. She's worried that Macbeth won't have the guts to carry out the murder. Okay, Clare? You be Lady Macbeth and I'll be everyone else."

At first I'm a wreck. I can't think. I know the part by heart but it isn't coming to me. Suddenly I think of Ginny Germain. I conjure up all her calm and confidence. I put the book down on the desk and pretend to be holding the letter from Macbeth in my hands.

> *"They met me in the day of success; and I have learned by the perfect'st report they have more in them than mortal knowledge. When I burned in desire to question them further, they made themselves air ..."*

Suddenly I'm flying, the words come to me magically and all I have to think about is the acting. I want the throne more than anything. I will spill as much blood as I have to to get it. Eric is stunned. He even forgets his line and I have to prompt him.

"Eric?"

"Uh-huh? Oh right, sorry. *The King comes here tonight.*"

I consider this before I respond.

> *"Thou'rt mad to say it:*
> *Is not thy master with him? who, were't so,*
> *Would have informed for preparation?"*

When we finish the act, the class claps and hoots and whistles. I blush deeply and Eric bows to me. I curtsy, holding out my imaginary skirts.

I try to hold on to the way it feels to be acting even for a few moments. I know that this is something I will think of forever when I think of the things that changed my life. Running is great, it's like flying. But this is a different kind of flying. It's like flying inside someone else's body.

Back at my locker, I'm Clare again. The combination on my lock isn't working. I try it about four more times until I glance up and realize I'm at the wrong locker. I shake my head, move over and try again. I want so much to share the last hour with someone. I glance over at Allison's locker. A tall, disgustingly handsome guy is leaning against her locker door. He looks about twenty, but he must be a ninth grader. Troy, I presume. Allison is smiling at him the way you do when you're falling hard for someone. After all the times Allison and I have whispered late into the night about the kind of boyfriends we'd want, this is the last guy I would expect to see her with. This is exactly, however, the kind of guy I'd expect to see Ginny Germain with.

As I'm thinking this, I see Ginny approaching from the end of the hall. She's watching Allison and Troy with pure evil in her eyes.

On the way home from school I notice that the air is changing just a little. It smells like half-summer and half-Halloween. The leaves have started to turn colour, and some of them spin slowly to the ground. I stop for a second to watch a squirrel run up the side of a tree, just like Spider-Man, chattering at me the whole way. From around the corner I hear someone screaming. The voice is unmistakable.

I turn the corner to find Patience spinning airplane-style around a kid about four times her size who is clutching her by her tiny ankle and wrist. I've seen this kid at the Dairy Delite. He's a real Neanderthal. He's laughing and he seems to be enjoying himself. Patience is screaming and crying. I can see angry red welts forming where he's gripping her. I can only imagine what Patience must have done or said to provoke this bully.

"Hey, put her down!" I yell.

He looks at me, unfazed. "Make me," he says, like a true Neanderthal.

I don't have many options; he's a lot bigger than me. He must be getting dizzy. I could wait him out until he's too dizzy to spin anymore, but Patience looks absolutely terrified. I decide to rush him. In the flurry of arms and legs that follows, Patience's foot nails me squarely in the right eye. The dizzy caveman stumbles to the ground and lets go of Patience, who sails through the air and hits the grass with a thump. She gets to her feet and promptly starts kicking him in the head.

"Big, fat, stupid!"

"Patience, stop!" I say, rubbing my eye. I seem to be blinded.

The bully gets up with a grunt and saunters away like a lion who's finished toying with his prey. Patience rubs her wrist and looks down at her swollen ankle. I stand up, still holding my hand over my eye. I can feel an egg growing on my cheekbone.

"Let's see," she demands.

I take my hand away.

"You're going to have a shiner," she says. "I had one once, too, or twice."

I put my backpack on my shoulders and head for my house. Patience is right on my heels.

"Wanna see my fish?" she says.

"Not right now," I say. "I have to ice my eye."

She shrugs and skips ahead of me, forgetting all about her sore ankle. I suddenly feel very sorry for her. It's obvious that she's used to being bullied, having people push her around, hurt her. She's so used to it that she thinks it's part of her daily life. She expects it.

"Hey, Patience," I say when we reach the end of her driveway.

She stops skipping and turns around. "What?"

"Don't let people push you around like that, okay? When someone tries to hurt you, just run home, okay?"

"You mean run like a horse or run like a dog?" she asks. She demonstrates a horse cantering, then a dog running on all fours.

I sigh and cross the street to my house.

Ironically, when I walk into the house, my mom is exercising to a Tae Bo DVD in the living room, punching her fist into the face of her imaginary enemy. When she sees me holding my hand over my eye, she shrieks and runs over to me, leaving Billy Blanks on the screen ducking and swinging alone. She pulls my hand off my eye and sits me down on the sofa.

"Mom, the DVD."

"Oh, right." She grabs the remote and clicks it off. "What happened?" She sits down next to me. "Wait, don't tell me yet." She runs into the kitchen and comes back with a bag of frozen peas, which she slaps on my face. "Hold that there. Now, what happened?"

"Patience was in trouble. A caveman was trying to launch her into space. I tried to help her but I got kicked."

"What caveman?" she demands. "Where does he live?"

"I'm guessing a cave?"

"Do you know this boy?"

"No. I've seen him around but we don't exactly travel in the same circles."

"Who are his parents?"

"His parents are wolves. Mom, can we just drop it? It was Patience who kicked me and it was an accident."

She looks at me and slowly shakes her head. Then she kisses my forehead. "Well, you're very brave. Do you know that?"

"Uh-huh, I get that a lot." I roll my eyes at her.

"Does it hurt?"

I shrug. "Some, but not that much."

"Can you see?"

I pull the bag of peas off my eyes. "Yup."

Later, on the roof, I'm lying on my back, looking up at the sky, thinking about all the things that have happened to me in the last few days. I wish Allison were here to talk about them with me. I sure wouldn't mind listening to some of her inside-track stories either. Elsie has licked my eye a thousand times with her big pink tongue, and I know that dog spit will probably heal it faster than anything. I close my eyes for a minute and relive the moment when the class cheered at my Lady Macbeth. When I open them, Elsa is sitting across from me, cross-legged.

"Yeah, it was pretty great, wasn't it?" she says.

"What?"

"Whaddya think? The foot in the eye? Lady Macbeth, you boobsky."

"Oh, yeah. I don't have the part yet, though. Who knows how many people will try out for it."

"I'm liking your chances." She winks at me. "Listen, Clare, I checked my schedule for next week and I've got some openings. You want me to run some lines with you?"

"Run some lines? How do you know about that stuff?"

"Let's just say that I've spent a little time in New York lately. Off-Broadway, of course. Well, actually more like off-off-Broadway."

I smile. "Sure, of course I'd like some help. Elsie's getting really sick of playing Macbeth. She keeps running away."

"I like where you're going with this acting stuff. Running is so boring."

"I'm not giving up running yet. I have to maintain my girlish figure."

Elsa looks at my eye. "Nice shiner. Can't wait to see it tomorrow."

I groan.

"Here," says Elsa, "take these." She hands me a pair of dark sunglasses that she's been wearing on top of her head.

"Thanks," I say, trying them on.

"Don't mention it. They were a gift from a French industrialist I met in Paris, and that is *so* over. By the way, you look fabulous in them, very mysterious."

I look up at the sky through the dark lenses. When I look back at Elsa, she's gone.

# Chapter 9

*"What hath quench'd them hath given me fire."*
LADY MACBETH

When you have a black eye, people are instantly nicer to you. It's important to take advantage of the situation. My mom made me an apple pie for dessert, and my dad actually made it home in time to eat dinner with us, which happens about as often as the vernal equinox. My dad was all over the black eye, threatening lawsuits and police action till my mom gave him a look. Somewhere along the way my mom has figured out that if things are going to work between us, she's going to have to stop making a big deal out of everything (she did make me take off the dark sunglasses at the table, though). My dad hasn't quite caught on to the program yet. He has two gears: high and asleep.

While my mom serves up the pie, my dad asks the usual questions.

"How are things at school?"

"Great."

"How's the running? Are you still making good time?"

"I guess, but I'm sort of interested in acting this year."

"You're giving up the track team?" He looks mildly concerned (he wanted a boy).

"I'm still taking Track and Field as a class, but I just want to focus on Drama right now. I'm auditioning for Lady Macbeth at the end of the week."

"Lady Macbeth? Now there's a motivated woman for you. Too bad she goes nuts in the end. The pressure just gets to be too much, I guess." He sighs and takes a sip of coffee.

My mom jumps in. "At least she doesn't lose her head literally. Nothing much has changed in the world. The women do all the thinking and the men do all the fighting."

My dad grunts, which is his standard reaction to a point when he doesn't want to incite a "discussion."

"Did you know that some people think there's a curse on that play?" asks my mom.

"A curse? What do you mean?" I say.

"I'm a little fuzzy on the details, but a lot of productions of the play have been plagued with catastrophes and, um, people dying and being stabbed and set on fire and stuff like that." Her voice trails off as she catches my dad looking at her in alarm.

"Honey, ignore your mom. She doesn't know what she's talking about. It's all just a bunch of theatre folklore."

"Oh, wait. I just remembered," says my mom. "You can avoid the curse by never saying the name of the play in the theatre it's performed in."

"But I already did!"

"Okay. Never mind then. How's that pie taste?"

"How do you guys know so much about *Macbeth*?" I ask.

"I played one of the witches in my college's production," says my mom. "Your dad must have seen the play seventeen times, didn't you, honey?"

My dad clears his throat. "Uh, that isn't entirely true. Most of the time I stayed for your first scene and then went for a couple of beers and came back for the end."

"I know," says my mom. "I always saw you leave. I was just testing you."

"What do you mean 'testing me'? Why do I need to be tested?"

"You don't. I was just checking to see if you could tell the truth after all these years."

"Of course I can. What difference does it make at this point anyway?"

I put my sunglasses on and sit back in my chair with my arms crossed. My mom notices and snaps out of it. My dad looks ready for round two.

"More pie, Clare?" asks my mom in an artificially sweetened voice.

"No, thanks."

My mom glares at my dad and he tries to get back to his line of questioning.

"What happened to that kid you used to hang out with?"

"Who?" I pretend not to know who he's talking about.

"You know, the smart one."

"Allison," says my mom icily. "Her name is Allison."

"No, that's not it. This was a boy. It was Peter, or something with a 'P.'"

"Paul?" I say. "You're talking about Paul? Dad, Paul's been gone for months. He left in July!"

"Oh, right, so Allison is your new friend. Got it. She's the one who left all those messages on the machine the other night."

"What messages?" I ask, alarmed.

"You didn't get those? Let's see, it was that night you went out with Aunt Rusty. Was that Saturday night? Yeah, you went to that poetry bash thing."

"Poetry slam! Dad, how could you not tell me about the messages?"

He shrugs. "I don't know. I just thought you got them."

I look at my mom. "Don't look at me," she says. "I never heard them."

I go into the kitchen, leaving them to argue about who dropped the ball on the parenting skills this time. I press the messages button on the answering machine. It says there are twelve saved messages and starts playing them.

"Hi, Clare, it's Allison. Look, I think we could have some fun at this party tonight. A few laughs anyway. I get why you don't want to go, but you can be my date. Get that party dress out of the mothballs and I'll pick you up at eight. Call me. Bye."

*<beep>*

"Hey, Clare, me again. It's seven-thirty and I'm leaving soon. Do me a favour and call me even if you don't want to go. I just want to talk to you, okay? Bye."

*<beep>*

"Hey, me again. This is the last time I'm calling. I mean it. Call me back. If you don't, I'm just going to go to that party and you'll be sorry. Bye."

*<beep>*

"Okay, really, I mean it. Last chance for romance … really. Bye."

I picture myself sitting in front of my therapist in twenty years explaining that my dad ruined my life because he doesn't know how to work an answering machine. He can run a corporation from his briefcase, but pass on a message? Forget about it.

It's too late to call Allison and say, "Hey, I got your message and …"

Too much water has gone under the bridge; that ship has sailed; my goose is cooked. I decide that the best possible way to deal with this is to approach Allison at school the next day, tell her what happened and just see where it goes from there.

Later, when I'm staring up at the ceiling in my bedroom, reviewing life's latest catastrophe, a chill runs through me when I think about the fortune teller and how she told me that the misunderstanding was partly my fault. In fact, come to think of it, a lot of things she told me that night have come true. Which reminds me of the three witches in *Macbeth*. Macbeth listens to them and gets himself into a horrible mess. I try to remember what else that crazy woman told me. Didn't she say what's broken shall be fixed? Does that mean I'm in charge of fixing it or will it fix itself? And what about this curse my mom told me about? Should I be afraid for my life?

Elsie is lying on the carpet next to my bed. She's having one of her cat-chasing dreams where her paws move and she woofs quietly. I shake her and she wakes with a start. She looks around and rolls over. I give her belly a scratch.

"Elsie, help me out here. What am I going to say tomorrow?"

Elsie puts her paw on my hand, which either means "Scratch me some more right there" or "Don't worry, you'll think of something." A dog's life is so uncomplicated.

# Chapter 10

The next day I decide to walk to school again. Note to self: buy more black turtlenecks and black headbands (and possibly a black car so I don't arrive at school all sweaty). My dark glasses add another element of mystery to the new me. I ignore the predictable comments in the hallways — "Hey, who died?"; "Where's the funeral?" — and head for my locker. Apparently the hours I spent awake last night formulating the perfect opening to approach Allison with were a complete waste of time because she isn't at her locker and she doesn't appear to be at school at all. I shuffle off to homeroom wondering what happened to her.

As I pass the memo board outside my homeroom, I notice a large fluorescent green memo with ATTENTION: STUDENT BODY written at the top. I stop to read it. It's from Principal Davidson and it's dated today.

## EFFECTIVE IMMEDIATELY

CELL PHONES WILL NO LONGER BE PERMITTED ON SCHOOL PROPERTY. THE STAFF AND I APOLOGIZE FOR ANY INCONVENIENCE THIS MAY CAUSE.

THERE IS A PAY TELEPHONE NEXT TO THE STAFF ROOM
AND ANOTHER ONE OUTSIDE THE GYMNASIUM.
IF YOU NEED TO MAKE AN EMERGENCY PHONE CALL
AND YOU DON'T HAVE A QUARTER,
PLEASE CONTACT THE OFFICE.

WE REGRET HAVING TO ENFORCE THIS NEW RULE,
BUT CELL PHONES HAVE BECOME A DISTRACTION TO
STUDENTS, AND THEY ARE INTERFERING WITH THE
TEACHING OF CLASSES.

Scrawled jaggedly across the bottom in what looks like red lipstick are the words *That means you, Ginny Germain!!!*

I gulp and look around. Is there an anarchist in our midst? A troublemaker? A rabble-rouser? I can't imagine who could have written that. I had no idea that someone else in eighth grade feels like I do about Ginny. I thought everyone admired her or at least feared her. Then it occurs to me that if Ginny sees this, she might assume I did it. In fact, she most certainly will assume I did it. Yikes. I watch the hallways empty into homerooms for a minute, then wipe my hand across the graffiti. It smears into a big red stain but is still totally readable, and now my hand is covered in red something.

I dash to the girls' bathroom and push open the door. If I were a cartoon character, my hair would be standing straight up. Ginny Germain is at the sink washing a red stain, identical to mine, off her hand. She must have found another graffitied memo. If this mysterious graffiti artist hit every memo, they will be all over the school, which means the writer could be from any grade. Ginny glares at me. I hide my hand behind my back and quickly lock myself in a stall. I sit on the toilet lid and wait. I think about Lady Macbeth washing her hands over and over, trying to wash away the blood from the grisly murders her husband has committed. Could this be a sign that Ginny is up to something awful? Hmmm. If I apply my "What-would-Lady-Macbeth-do?" mantra to the situation, the deed is already done.

By the time Ginny leaves and I finally get the red stuff off my hand, I'm late for homeroom. Skulking to the back of the class is not an option when you walk in alone and late. Mrs. Sneider can't help but make a big deal over the dark glasses.

"Clare, will you please remove your sunglasses," she says, all pinched and disapproving.

I look right at her and slide my sunglasses far enough down my nose so that she can see the black eye.

"Or keep them on. Whatever works for you."

Of course I know what's next. Mrs. Sneider snags me on my way out the door at the end of homeroom.

"Clare, can I talk to you for a moment?"

"Sure," I say, fake-glancing at the clock above the door.

"Clare, are you all right?" she asks. "What happened to your eye, dear?"

I sigh. "I got kicked by a little girl I was playing with, that's all."

She still looks skeptical. "Is everything all right at home?"

"You mean, are my parents beating me?"

"Well, no, I ..." she fumbles. "I was just concerned."

"No. They're crazy but they're not child-beaters. Can I go now?"

"Sure."

I dash to my next class, narrowly missing Eric, who is walking in the opposite direction. Actually not so much walking as sauntering. Why is it that he's never in a hurry? He smiles and pretends that I've spun him around.

"Sorry," I say.

"Nice shades. Those new?" he asks.

"Sort of," I answer, walking backward. "I've got a shiner." I show him.

"Sheesh, tell me you got at least one good punch in."

I grin. "Sure I did." Then I dash off down the hallway.

He calls after me, "Hey, are you ready for Friday?"

I turn around and give him a confident thumbs-up, but my stomach does a backflip.

In the cafeteria at lunchtime I start scoping out the student body, looking for clues. Ginny is at her usual table with her usual entourage. I pretend to be reading a poetry collection by Leonard Cohen that I stole from my mom's bookshelf. From where I'm sitting at the very back of the cafeteria, I've got a clear view of Ginny and anyone in the room who might be looking at her funny. The black sunglasses are indispensable for spying. Suddenly my ears perk up at a conversation going on between a couple of ninth-grade girls at the very next table. I keep my eyes glued to the poetry and listen hard.

The blonde girl moves in a little closer to her friend and looks around. "It was definitely someone at the party. Someone must have just walked into Troy's mom's room and taken it out of her jewellery box. His mom's bedroom is right next to the bathroom."

The other girl shakes her head. "But who would do that? We know everyone who was there."

"We do, don't we? Except …"

"Except who?" asks the brunette.

"Well, that new eighth grader, Allison. No one knows her too well. Didn't Ginny bring her to the party?"

The brunette thinks about it. "I think so, but Troy seems to have a thing for Allison, and I don't think Ginny's too happy about it. Anyway, she's awfully nice. I really don't think she would steal a necklace out of Troy's mom's jewellery box, do you?"

The blonde looks around. "Does anyone really ever know anyone?" she asks with a raised eyebrow. "All I know is that Troy's mom told him he has to talk to everyone who was there that night and see if he can get it back, and if he can't she's going to report it to the police as a robbery."

I gulp for the second time that day. My Spidey-Senses are tingling. My heart is pounding. I look over at Ginny, who is delicately picking green grapes off a cluster and putting them, one by one, into her mouth. I smell a rat.

Later, as I'm crossing the staff parking lot headed for home, I see Troy and Ginny standing between two cars, talking. I duck behind a pickup truck and peek through the windows at them. Troy is talking with his hands and looking very upset. He scratches his forehead and runs his fingers through his hair as though he doesn't believe something she's telling him. Ginny is shaking her head slowly, looking very fake sincere. She puts her arm around Troy's shoulders as though to comfort him, but he doesn't look at all comforted. He looks distraught. I wait until they walk away before I stand up, feeling a lot like one of those crime-scene investigators from TV. I walk home in a daze, trying to figure out what the heck is going on.

Patience isn't at her usual post and I look around, concerned. I assume she's got herself in some kind of trouble, but I'm torn between making a run for it to the safety of my house or finding out if she's okay. As I'm deliberating, the green Volvo pulls into the driveway and her mom gets out. She walks around and opens the passenger door for Patience, which seems odd to me. Patience is not her spring-loaded self. She gets out of the car carefully and then I see that her right arm is encased in a bright purple cast. All I can think is that she managed to defy death again. When Patience sees me she instantly perks up.

"Hey, hi! Look at my arm. The doctor said I could have purple, red or green and of course I took purple."

"Hi, Patience," I say warily. "What happened to your arm?"

"It broke," she says.

"How'd it break?" I ask. Patience's mother goes inside the house. She looks exhausted.

"Carrie told me to jump off the roundabouts," she says. "Doesn't hurt, though."

"Patience," I say, "would you like to look at my comic book collection?"

Her face lights up and she nods with her whole body. After I clear it with her mom, we start to walk across the street together. I grab Patience by the collar of her shirt and pull her back onto the curb as she almost walks into an oncoming car.

# Chapter 11

*"What's done cannot be undone."*
LADY MACBETH

I finally send Hurricane Patience home and try to put my post-apocalyptic bedroom back together. My mom gets an assist for bringing in a plate of sugar cookies. (Why stop there? Why not whip her up a double espresso?) I know she means well, but she needs to understand that Patience can convert sugar into energy faster than you can say, "Hey, get down off that dresser." You'd think a broken arm would slow her down, but you'd be wrong.

I use what little energy I have left to work on my Lady Macbeth lines, but I'm having trouble concentrating. I want to call Allison and ask her if she's okay or just talk to her. I pick up the phone and dial her number but then hang up. I dial again and let it ring once before I hang up. That's as far as I get. I call Aunt Rusty instead and catch her in a bad mood. I get the feeling that things aren't going so well with her and Mr. Bianchini because when I ask about him she says, "Who?" Needless to say, she's no help at all. I try to conjure Elsa but she doesn't materialize, and I imagine her off at some elegant party somewhere. I end up going to bed after dinner, exhausted, confused and alone.

The next morning at school I see Allison at her locker, looking very pale. Maybe she really was sick. I decide to seize the moment and head down the hallway to her locker to talk to her, but I see Ginny approaching from the opposite direction and hang back, pretending to read a flyer on the bulletin board about tryouts for the gymnastics club (yup, I am *so* interested). I keep one eye on Ginny as she approaches Allison, all full of fake concern. Allison nods a few times and then puts her backpack in her locker. She slams her locker shut and heads off to homeroom as Ginny waves goodbye. Ginny is fiddling with the lock on her own locker, but she's also watching Allison walk away. I hide behind a propped-open door and watch Ginny through the glass.

As soon as Allison is out of sight I see Ginny move one locker over, to Allison's, dial the combination and open it. She looks around, then takes something shiny out of the pocket of her jeans and unzips the front pocket of Allison's backpack. She drops the thing in her hand into Allison's pack and zips it shut. Then she slams the locker door, locks it and heads down the hallway, away from her homeroom. As soon as she's far enough away I follow her, staying close to the walls. I peek around the corner and there she is, talking on the pay phone with a gym sock over the mouthpiece. I can't get close enough to hear what she's saying, but the call only lasts a couple of minutes. Before Ginny spies me, I bolt back down the hallway and duck into my homeroom, completely out of breath.

Mrs. Sneider looks at me, startled. "Clare, this is becoming a habit."

"Sorry," I pant. "I just got a little lost … or something."

Mrs. Sneider looks at me and shakes her head. "Please sit down, dear. You're disrupting homeroom."

I walk to my desk, avoiding the eyes of my classmates. To them, I'm too much of a geek to be drawing all this attention. Out of the corner of my eye I can see them exchanging unamused glances.

As soon as I get settled, Principal Davidson's voice comes over the intercom. "Would Allison Truman please come to the office. Allison Truman."

My hand flies up in the air. Right in the middle of roll call. Mrs. Sneider ignores me.

"Mrs. Sneider?" I say, interrupting her. "I need to be excused."

"Young lady, you've just arrived. What's this all about?"

"I don't feel so good," I say, moving my hand to my stomach. This always works. All teachers fear potential barfing.

"All right. Go," she says, looking a bit skeptical. But I'm already gone.

I dash down the empty hallway to the office, skidding to a halt in front of the glass window that looks into Principal Davidson's office. Allison is sitting in a chair across from him, looking stricken. I dash back down the hallway to Allison's locker. Darn! Why didn't I learn her combination?

I try her birthdate first. It won't open. My fingers are shaking. I try her house address, her birth year. I'm starting to panic. Then it comes to me. Her phone number. I try the first three numbers and the lock clicks open. I open the locker and unzip the front pocket of Allison's backpack. I feel a chain, pull it out and stuff it into my pocket. Down the hallway I can see Allison and Principal Davidson walking toward me. Allison is looking at the floor. I slip into the girls' bathroom, which is empty, but not for long. Homeroom ends in three minutes. I lock myself in a stall and pull the necklace out of my pocket. It's a long, delicate gold chain with a big teardrop-shaped diamond at the end of it. I put it back in my pocket.

As soon as I hear the bell to end homeroom, I leave the bathroom and walk to Allison's locker, where Principal Davidson is still looking through Allison's things. He's looking more and more embarrassed at finding nothing. Allison is looking around, horrified at the crowd that's gathering. Ginny is nowhere to be seen. I walk up to Principal Davidson and ask him if I can have a moment of his time in private. He notices how serious I look and says okay. I tell him that I think Allison should come along. I wink at her but she's too confused to respond. Principal Davidson walks back to the office with us. He closes the door and we sit down.

"Now, what's this all about?"

I pull the necklace out of my pocket. "I think this is what you're looking for."

He looks at it. Allison looks at it.

"Where did you get that?" he asks.

"I took it out of Allison's backpack," I say.

"Wait a second," says Allison. "I never ..."

"I know you didn't take it," I say. "I saw Ginny Germain plant it in your backpack before homeroom this morning."

Principal Davidson takes the necklace from me. "I'm sorry, but I have to ask you this. Have you ever been inside Troy Buckley's house?"

"No," I say. "I don't even know Troy."

Principal Davidson rubs his chin for a second, then picks up the microphone for the school loudspeaker and says, "Ginny Germain and Troy Buckley to the principal's office, please." He looks at us, thinking a second. "Why don't you two wait outside while I talk to Ginny and Troy. I'll keep the necklace."

Allison and I leave the office and sit on the wooden bench in the hallway. Allison looks at me as if she's about to say something. I want to tell her that it's okay, it was nothing. She leans in a bit closer, looking into my eyes.

"What the heck happened to your eye?" she says. "You look like Rocky Balboa after twelve rounds!"

"Oh." I touch the lump on my cheekbone. "Long story."

Just then Ginny walks past us, and even though I know she sees us, she doesn't make eye contact. Troy approaches from the opposite hallway, looking bewildered.

We should pretend we're ignoring what's going on in the office, but what else are we going to do? We turn ourselves around on the bench and watch through the glass windows. Principal Davidson asks Ginny a few questions and her normally confident face starts to crumble. Troy's face, on the other hand, goes from confusion to clarity to rage as he finally puts all the pieces of the puzzle together. He stands up and starts yelling things at Ginny, who seems to shrink into herself.

Principal Davidson calls us back into his office, where Ginny looks on the verge of tears. There aren't any more chairs, so we stand. Troy looks sheepishly at Allison. He tells her that he never wanted to believe Ginny when she told him that she saw Allison take the necklace at the party that night (so that's what she was telling him in the parking lot yesterday). Allison appears unmoved. Principal Davidson makes Ginny apologize to Allison right before he suspends her for two weeks. Ha!

Everyone is dismissed from the office except Ginny. I expect Allison to go off with Troy somewhere, but she waves to him and catches up with me instead.

"Hey, wait up," she says.

I stop and wait for her. "I told you not to go to that party."

"You did, didn't you," she says. "What made you want to save my butt?"

I shrug. "I dunno. That's what friends do for each other."

"Yeah," she says. "I guess it is. Thanks. Hey, let me know the next time you need me to take a bullet or slay a dragon for you or bail you out of jail or drive the getaway car or give you a kidney, okay?"

"Sure. Let's hope it never comes to that." I smile at her and suddenly I feel like I know her again.

Later, I'm lying on the roof, watching a huge, orange harvest moon bob in front of me like a giant pumpkin. I close my eyes and rerun the highlight reel of the day in my head for the hundredth time, except this time I run it in slow motion with the *Chariots of Fire* soundtrack in the background. I feel like Spider-Man after a full day of fighting crime. I envision a tickertape parade and majorettes carrying a banner with CLARE SAVES THE DAY written on it, followed by lunch with the mayor where he presents me with a plaque for bravery (not to mention catlike reflexes and precision timing). I start writing my acceptance speech in my head.

"Ahem."

I open my eyes. Elsa is sitting cross-legged in front of me, staring at me. She's wearing a T-shirt with Charlie Chaplin on the front. Her hair is in braids.

"Oh, there you are. I wasn't sure when you'd be back from your ego trip."

"Me? Where were you yesterday when I needed you?"

"Sorry about that. I had to christen a boat, well, a ship, actually."

"A ship? What's it called?"

"I wanted to call it *The Minnow* but no one thought that was funny. They named it *The Princess Heloise*." She makes a face. "But that's not really important right now. The important thing is that you were brilliant today, absolutely brilliant."

"Thanks."

"Hey, how do you think Ginny's taking all this?"

I consider the question. "Not very well, I bet. In fact, she probably wants to kill me."

"I wouldn't worry about that. She's in enough trouble already. So, how do you figure out someone like Ginny?"

I shrug. "I don't know, I guess it's greed. She wants everything. That kind of thing is bound to catch up with you sooner or later."

"Wow. Just like Lady Macbeth," muses Elsa. "Spooky."

"The similarities are becoming painfully obvious, aren't they?"

"Yeah, maybe art does imitate life."

"Hmmm," I say. "Look at that moon."

Elsa turns around and lies down on the shingles next to me, looking up at the sky. "It's beautiful. It looks like a perfect *crème brûlée*."

"It looks like endless possibilities," I say.

# Chapter 12

My mom thinks that Aunt Rusty talks to me about inappropriate things, and she's absolutely right. That's why I like hanging out with her. I think that my aunt looks at me and sees a twenty-six-year-old even though she knows I'm only thirteen. At least, I think she knows.

We're eating dinner at an Indian restaurant that both of us like a lot. It's in a section of the city that's filled with Greek, Italian, Indian and Chinese restaurants. I love coming here because it's so mysterious. Every alleyway seems to hold a secret, and every doorway emits its own pungent aroma. People on the sidewalks yell at each other in foreign languages and carry colourful shopping bags filled with strange fruits and vegetables. Aunt Rusty and I are sipping mango *lassis* and nibbling on *naan* while we wait for our curries. Sitar music is playing softly in the background.

I've just finished filling her in on the drama of the last few days of my life, which I think is more exciting than anything on television — not to mention it stars *me*! I'm not getting the reaction I'm looking for. Not one "Wow!" She's distracted and agitated. I ask her if everything's okay.

"No," she says. "Everything's not okay. I think I want to break up with Len."

"Why?" I ask, remembering that I've waited for this

moment forever. Now that it's here, I feel completely in-different. In fact, the last time I had Track-and-Field class, I couldn't wait for it to be over. I barely even noticed Mr. Bianchini was there. Hmmm.

"I don't know," says Aunt Rusty, rubbing her temples. "It's just not working. I'm not happy. I don't think he's happy. Do you think he's happy?"

I shrug. "I don't know. I'm not sure what happy looks like on him."

"That's what I'm talking about!" she says. "I can't tell either!"

"Well, I never really thought you had a whole lot in common to begin with."

"I know," Aunt Rusty says, her face sliding through her hands. She lays her head on the table. "Why didn't you tell me?"

"Tell you what?" I ask.

"That it was a purely physical attraction and it would be over in three months."

"I didn't know that. I only started wearing a bra two months ago. I really don't know much about that stuff."

Aunt Rusty lifts her head up and looks at me. "No. Of course you don't. I'm sorry. Will you break up with him for me?"

The Indian waiter arrives with our curries. He sets them over tiny candles and places a bowl of fragrant rice in front of each of us.

I wait till he disappears again. "Maybe he'll break up

with you. Maybe he's at a restaurant tonight, just like you, trying to figure out how to do it. I bet he's not asking his thirteen-year-old niece to do it for him."

"What can I say? I'm a coward. I'm an awful person."

"No. You just don't want to hurt him."

"Yeah. Oh, wait! Maybe I'll give him that painting of mine that he likes so much."

"What are you going to say? Here's a lovely parting gift? It's a relationship, not a game show."

"You're right. Besides, his television is bigger than the painting. It's revolting. If you own a big-screen TV, you forfeit your right to own art. There ought to be a law that says your TV can't be bigger than your art."

"Mr. Bianchini has a big-screen TV?"

"Enormous. It's like the athletes are actually in there."

"What does he watch?"

Aunt Rusty sighs. "I dunno, any sport that ends with the word 'ball.' Never get involved with a man, okay?"

"Sure," I say, digging into my *saag*. "You can drop me off at a convent on the way home. I'm sure it will be a very fulfilling life."

Aunt Rusty laughs for the first time that night. Thankfully, she changes the subject. I've managed to keep the thought of Aunt Rusty's and Mr. Bianchini's physical relationship out of my brain till now, but if she continues like this it might start to seep in, and then there would be *saag* everywhere.

"When's the audition?" she asks.

"Tomorrow."

"Should you be out? Shouldn't you be at home getting ready?"

"I'm already ready. Besides, a person's gotta eat."

"True. Now give me your best Lady Macbeth."

I put down my fork and sit up straight.

> *Infirm of purpose!*
> *Give me the daggers."*

I pull a knife off the table and hold it up in the air.

> *"The sleeping and the dead*
> *Are but as pictures. 'Tis the eye of childhood*
> *That fears a painted devil. If he do bleed,*
> *I'll gild the faces of the grooms withal,*
> *For it must seem their guilt."*

Aunt Rusty claps and I bow my head.

"Excellent! You really got to me! Now hand me the chutney."

As I hand her the bowl of sticky mango chutney I wonder if it's a mistake to be so confident. I'm used to being filled with self-doubt and anxiety. It seems strange to be self-assured about something I've never even done before.

"So I guess you and Allison are back to being pals again?" she asks, spooning chutney onto her plate.

"Well. Sort of. I think it's important not to rush back into things. I mean, I kept her out of prison and all, but we need some time to think about things and heal."

"Clare, listen to yourself. You sound like some kind of new-age evangelist."

"I do not."

"Yeah, you do. You want some advice? Forgive, forget, hug, move on. Have fun."

"Move on? That's pretty big talk for someone who's afraid to break up with her boyfriend."

Aunt Rusty licks chutney off her finger and looks thoughtful.

Later, in bed with Elsie lying across my feet snoring away, I think about what Aunt Rusty told me at the restaurant. She's right. Why do I have to analyze everything to death? I should be enjoying myself. I decide that, starting tomorrow, I'll live every minute of my life to the fullest. That is, every minute following the audition, which is making me extremely nervous now that I'm alone in the dark. In fact, I'm feeling a bit nauseated. I hope it isn't something I ate.

## Chapter 13

At 4:00 a.m. I kick the covers off and lie there, spread-eagled. I'm hot and sweaty and my stomach has moved from its regular place to somewhere up near the back of my throat. I make a dash for the bathroom and get there just in time to eject the *saag* into the toilet. My mom shows up two split seconds later and I'm glad because vomiting is so much fun that one should never do it alone. She holds my hair out of my face and wets a washcloth at the same time, demonstrating brilliant multi-tasking. She hands me the washcloth and then runs downstairs to get ginger ale. As for me, I vomit until there's nothing left and then lay my cheek against the cool porcelain edge of the bathtub and put the wet cloth over my face.

My mom returns with a bucket and ginger ale and helps me into bed. I try to explain that the bathroom floor is better, so cool and convenient to the toilet, but she thinks I'm delirious with fever. Once I'm in bed again, she wets me down with a new cloth and gives me tiny sips of ginger ale between high-speed trips back to the bathroom. I feel as though I've vomited not only tonight's dinner but the last three months of dinners as well.

I sleep on and off. When I do sleep, a chaotic nightmare featuring a queen, a sitar player and Mr. Bianchini runs through my head like a bad movie. The queen isn't Lady Macbeth; she's the Queen of Hearts from a playing card. She's sitting across from me at the Indian restaurant and she whispers to me over and over that the *Macbeth* curse has been unleashed. Mr. Bianchini puts a plate of chicken *tikka masala* in front of me. He's wearing gym shorts and sneakers. There's a stopwatch and a whistle on a cord around his neck. The sitar player is wearing the same outfit. He sits on the floor plucking at his instrument. I inhale the aroma of the food in front of me and run for the bathroom but, of course, my legs are dream legs and heavy as cement. Luckily I wake up in time to make it to the real bathroom. Could the Queen of Hearts be right? Have I been cursed?

At 6:00 a.m. my dad gets up. He stands in the doorway of my bedroom, where I'm lying, ghostlike, with my mom passed out next to me.

"Morning!" he says, all chipper and awake, as he ties his tie.

My mom sits up and rubs her eyes. She looks at me and puts her hand on my forehead.

"Are you feeling better?" she asks.

I nod, remembering that I've got to get to the auditions this afternoon, but my stomach is twisted up like a pretzel.

My dad must have slept through the whole thing because he asks what's wrong with me.

"Nothing," I say. "I must have eaten something poisonous but I'm fine now, really. I should get up and get in the shower."

"Super," says my dad, already on his way downstairs.

"You're positively grey," says my mom. "You're not going anywhere."

"But I have my audition today!" I plead.

"We'll see. You try to get a little sleep and I'll make you some dry toast and tea. Then we'll talk."

Elsie follows her down the stairs and they leave me alone. I do some quick math. The auditions start at three. That's almost nine hours away. I should be fine by then.

I get up and hobble weakly to the bathroom. The cramps in my belly are so bad that I have to limp. I look at myself in the bathroom mirror. The only colour I have in my face is the greenish-purple bruise around my left eye. Great. I take the phone from my mom's room and smuggle it back into bed with me. I dial Allison's number. Her mom answers and puts Allison on. I can hear her yawning.

"Allison, it's Clare."

"What time is it?" She yawns again.

"Never mind that. I'm in trouble. I've got my Lady Macbeth audition today and I've been hurling my guts out all night."

"Gross."

"Does that sound familiar?" I ask.

"Yup. Been there, done that."

"Do you think I have what you had?"

"I dunno. I definitely had the nonstop hurling."

"Check. What else?"

"Let me see. I was hot, sweaty, feverish."

"Check, check, check."

"That's about it, except for the explosive diarrhea."

"Wait, what?"

"Oh, you don't have it yet? I'd stay close to a bathroom if I were you."

"How long till you were better?"

"Twenty-four hours, that's the good news. By this time tomorrow you'll be good as new."

"Yeah, except I need to be good as new today at three o'clock."

"Hmmm, that could be tricky."

"I need you to do me a favour, okay?"

"Sure. Ask away. I owe you big time. I don't have to donate a kidney, do I?"

"No. Go to the auditions in the Drama room at three o'clock. Tell Eric I might be a little late. Tell him I need to go last, okay?"

"Sure, that's easy, no problem. You want me to stall him? I can do that. I once pretended to faint to avoid a blood test."

"No, thanks. Probably not necessary. I'll get there as soon as I can. I guess I'll see you there."

"You bet. Good luck, Clare."

I hang up the phone and slide it under my bed. My mom arrives with a tray of tea and toast. She jams a thermometer in my mouth and looks at me anxiously.

"Where did you go for dinner last night?"

"Ahfoka Cuwwy Houf," I say, talking around the thermometer.

"Ashoka Curry House? Aunt Rusty said you were going for burgers."

"I wike dat pwace," I say.

She pulls the thermometer out and looks at it. "A hundred-point-six. You're still feverish."

"You think it was the Indian food?" I ask.

"I don't know, could be."

"But if it was the Indian food, I could be better soon, right? Sooner than if I had the flu."

"I don't know. Why don't you try to eat something? Make sure you keep sipping that water, too. You're probably dehydrated."

I spend the morning on the sofa, wrapped in a blanket, sipping water and watching TV with the attention span of a gnat, flipping channels from the juggler to the lady making moussaka to the dog show to the coin-collecting show to the cowboy movie to the evangelist to the soap opera and so on till I'm back at the beginning again. My mom checks on me every half hour while she tortures me with cooking smells in the kitchen. By noon my temperature is normal and I manage to drink some beef broth and eat a few soda crackers. I've got one eye on the clock and I'm still waiting for the diarrhea to kick in, but so far so good.

I call Aunt Rusty but she doesn't pick up. She's either out or sleeping or dead. I picture her curled around the toilet with no one to cool her forehead (I don't think it's appropriate to ask your boyfriend to stand by and hold your hair out of your face while you throw up when you're about to break up with him), and I'm really grateful for my mom.

At two, I hobble into the shower. Washing my hair is exhausting. I pull on the same clothes I was wearing last night, but the lingering smell of curry makes me feel nauseous again, so I stuff everything into the laundry hamper and start over. I end up in jeans and a green sweater that perfectly matches my eye. My mom puts a little blush on my cheeks, gives me some aspirin and some just-in-case Kaopectate, which tastes like dirt, and then she drives me to school. I won't let her come inside with me, so she heads to the grocery store after wishing me luck.

I move slowly through the empty halls, taking deep breaths to try to calm myself. I open the heavy door to the Drama room. Three girls are auditioning for the witch roles. They're all ninth graders. They chant, "*Fair is foul, and foul is fair. Hover through the fog and filthy air.*"

I scan the room for Eric. He's in the back holding a clipboard. Allison is standing right next to him. She waves at me. Ninth graders are scattered around the room in little groups, reading *Macbeth* and mouthing the words silently. When the witches are finished, Eric comes to the front of the room and Allison follows. Eric stops to ask me if I'm ready. I nod.

Allison looks at me closely. "You look a bit like death. Are you going to be okay?"

"I hope so. Thanks for waiting for me."

"No problem."

Eric announces that someone named Simon and I will be auditioning first for Macbeth and Lady Macbeth. A guy stands up and comes forward. He's rather tall with black, curly hair. I've seen him around with a very pretty girl named Sylvia, who is also rather tall with black, curly hair. They've always looked to me like one of those couples who have been together forever. They must have met when they were toddlers.

I move gingerly past Eric to the centre of the stage. He stops in front of me and says, "Gum." He holds out his hand.

"What?" I say, confused.

"Give me your gum."

I take the gum out of my mouth and put it in his hand. The weird thing is, I don't remember putting it *in* my mouth.

Eric winks at me and I transform myself into Lady Macbeth, a woman who would never chew Bazooka bubble gum.

# Chapter 14

Simon walks across the stage and joins me in the centre. I explain to my husband, who is falling apart, that he had better suck it up because we can't undo the horrible thing we've done. The king is dead.

> *"How now, my lord! why do you keep alone,*
> *Of sorriest fancies your companions making,*
> *Using those thoughts which should indeed have died*
> *With them they think on? Things without all remedy*
> *Should be without regard: what's done is done."*

Simon has a hint of a smile, which disappears as he transforms himself into Macbeth and unloads on me with his tortured thoughts.

> *"We have scotch'd the snake, not killed it:*
> *She'll close and be herself, whilst our poor malice*
> *Remains in danger of her former tooth.*
> *But let the frame of things disjoint, both the worlds suffer,*
> *Ere we will eat our meal in fear, and sleep*
> *In the affliction of these terrible dreams*
> *That shake us nightly: better be with the dead,*
> *Whom we, to gain our peace, have sent to peace,*
> *Than on the torture of the mind to lie*
> *In restless ecstasy. Duncan is in his grave."*

*"After life's fitful fever he sleeps well,*
*Treason has done his worst: nor steel nor poison,*
*Malice domestic, foreign levy, nothing,*
*Can touch him further."*

I take Macbeth's hands in mine, look him right in the eye and basically tell him to buck up 'cause we've got company for dinner.

*"Come on;*
*Gentle my lord, sleek o'er your rugged looks;*
*Be bright and jovial among your guests to-night."*

We continue on and finish the scene without a single mistake. Eric, who seemed to be holding his breath, suddenly exhales, puts his clipboard under his arm and claps like a madman. The rest of the room joins in. My husband, Macbeth, changes back to Simon, and I change back into a too-tall eighth grader with a black eye and a stomach in knots. I scan the room for Allison. She's in the back, clapping and whistling like a boy at a football game. Elsa is sitting right next to her, clapping like an aristocrat at a horse race. She waves at me like the Queen of England.

I tell Eric I have to leave. I notice he's chewing bubble gum.

"That's not my gum, is it?"

"Why?"

"I have the stomach flu."

He pretends to spit the gum out onto the floor. Then he looks at me deadpan. "No. It's not your gum. I happen to have my own gum."

As I walk out the door with Allison, he yells, "Postings on Monday morning outside the Drama room!"

Allison and I wait outside for my mom to pick us up.

"Wow, Clare, I didn't know you were such an … actress." She does her best femme fatale by looking up at the sky mournfully with the back of her hand draped across her forehead.

"Me neither. I just sort of took to it. Do you think I have a chance?" I concentrate on the toe of my sneaker.

"Sure, unless Meryl Streep auditions after you, I think you're in."

"Thanks," I say. "That means a lot to me."

"Hey, too bad you missed school today. It was sort of like 'Ding Dong, the Witch Is Dead' without Ginny Germain around. Things were almost relaxed."

"How typical. The first day of life without Ginny Germain and I miss it."

"I'm feeling pretty bad about all that. I'm sorry I didn't take your word for it when you told me to watch my back around her."

"I'm sorry, too. I acted like a child."

Just then my mom pulls up to the curb and we hop in. She asks me how it went and I fill her in. She drops Allison off at her house and I tell her I'll call her later.

At home my mom makes me get back on the sofa with a blanket. Elsie gets up with me. Thankfully we're in time to catch the last hour of kids' cartoons. My mom makes me chicken soup with saltines for dinner, and I get to eat in front of the TV on a TV tray.

The fact that I didn't see any of the other auditions makes me feel a little unsure of my chances for the role. Eric was really enthusiastic, but he's like that about everything. Then I think about something I haven't allowed myself to consider till now. If I get the part, I hope that Simon gets the role of Macbeth. That moment when I pulled him close and looked into his eyes — I know that was acting, but did I feel a connection? Nah, I must have imagined it. Maybe it was the fever. After all, I had a black eye and I looked like a corpse with undertaker's makeup. But isn't it true that they say actors have to have a certain "chemistry" to make it work?

After dinner I call Allison and we talk forever, just like we used to, only now it's like she's been away to a strange foreign country and she's reporting back to me about the customs and mating rituals of the natives. I grill her about Troy's party.

"Was everyone making out?" I ask.

"Well, I think I left before things really got going. My mom wanted me home by eleven. But I saw a lot of French kissing, which I think is sort of insulting to the French. It looked to me like it should be called 'Hey, let-me-see-if-I-can-fit-your-head-in-my-mouth' kissing."

"Gross."

"Oh, and the music! Don't get me started on that. Based on their taste in music alone, I could never be friends with these people. Really, Clare, I wish you had come. I needed you there."

"What about Troy?" I ask.

"What about him?"

"Well, he seems to really like you."

"Like me? He believed Ginny's lies without ever asking me my side of the story."

"Um, I think now would be a good time to tell you that I was spying on Ginny and Troy when Ginny told him that lie about the necklace."

"Really, and what did you discover, Nancy Drew?"

"Well, he really looked upset and he seemed like he wasn't buying her story."

"He never came to me. He should have come to me but he didn't. I can't forgive him for that."

"Okay. But let me just say this. Ginny is very convincing when she sets her mind on something or someone. She's just like Lady Macbeth. She'll stop at nothing."

"Troy shouldn't have let her intimidate him."

"Well, let's change the subject. Did he kiss you?"

"Troy?"

"No, Barney the Dinosaur. Of course Troy."

"Not at the party. Once I saw Ginny's eyes throwing daggers at me from across the room I thought I better lay low."

"But you did kiss him?"

"Well, yes."

"Location, please."

"You know that bench that overlooks the ravine behind the baseball diamonds?"

"Intimately," I say, remembering the night I finally found Elsie there with Elsa. "What was it like?"

"Hmmm. At first it was awkward and horrible, but then I relaxed and it was just …" She paused.

"What? It was just what?"

"Nice. It was nice. It gave me butterflies in the pit of my stomach. I couldn't understand the kids at the party slobbering all over each other when a simple kiss seems so much more meaningful." Allison sounds all dreamy but she suddenly snaps out of it. "Anyway, by tomorrow you're going to feel fine. You want to go to a movie or something?"

We decide to see *Annie Hall* at the Princess Theatre even though we've both seen it a few times. It's one of those movies you never get tired of.

After I hang up the phone, I try to envision Allison's first kiss. It seems so romantic that I feel incredibly jealous. I guess I wasn't counting on being left behind on the first-kiss milestone. But what was I thinking? Did I expect two perfect guys to materialize in front of us and say, "Hello, we're here to deliver your first kiss. Now, pucker up"?

I do know one thing, and that is that I need to find someone to kiss me. The sooner the better.

# Chapter 15

The world is a kinder place when you have a best friend. People are friendlier, your jokes are funnier and everything seems to move along happily, as it should, around the nucleus that is you and your best friend.

Allison and I ride the bus home together after the movie. Golden leaves are starting to accumulate in the gutters, and they make a wonderful crunching sound every time the bus pulls in to a stop. We have our knees up against the seat in front of us and we're trading stories the way Diane Keaton and Woody Allen do in *Annie Hall* because seeing the movie has made us feel sophisticated and smart. I'm doing my best neurotic actress for Allison.

"It's not the acting *per se*," I say, using my hands like Woody does. "It's the validation I'm looking for. When I was six I was the turkey in the Thanksgiving pageant and I kept yelling at the director, 'What's my motivation here?!' I needed to know. I mean, sure, I'm going to die, but how do I feel about that?"

Allison is in hysterics. "I know what you mean. I wouldn't let my mother put a sheet over me for Halloween and make me into a ghost until she explained to me *why* I was a ghost and the ghost of whom."

"Right. Exactly. Because a ghost is essentially an unhappy dead person. Don't just throw a sheet on me and say, 'Be a ghost.' I need to know who I am at this moment."

Allison snorts and blows a bubble with her gum. She looks out the window of the bus and nudges me.

"Isn't that your neighbour?" she asks.

"Where?"

"Right there." She points out the window and I strain to see over her.

Patience is running next to the bus wearing a red cape, a red helmet and red rubber boots with yellow ducks on them. The purple cast on her arm pokes out from under the cape. On her face is the determined look of a super-hero. The bus pulls away from the curb and Patience picks up the pace, her little legs struggling to keep up. I watch her get smaller for a few seconds and then bigger and bigger as the bus slows down again for a stop sign. Just as she gets close enough to touch the tail light of the bus, it takes off again. It occurs to me that this might be partially my fault since I gave her those superhero comic books to read.

"Let's get off at the next stop," I say.

Allison pulls the cord to ring the bell, and we gather up our packs and head to the exit in the middle of the bus. In a moment the bus hisses to a stop and the doors flap open. I jump out first and Patience comes at me from the right, slamming into me like a bowling ball. Allison picks her up off the grass as I try to recover my balance. Patience is still panting, but she seems all set to continue chasing the bus.

"Whoa, Patience," I say, tackling her. "Where ya going?"

"That bus is bad. It squashed a squirrel. I'm a crime fighter."

"Does your mom know where you are?" I ask, sounding frighteningly like one.

"Does yours?" asks Patience, hands on her hips.

Allison starts to laugh.

We're about three stops from home so we decide to walk rather than wait for the next bus. Besides, the idea of taking Patience on a bus is very unappealing.

We discover that the only way to make progress is to take Patience prisoner. Allison holds one of her hands and I clutch the purple cast on the other side. People passing us on the sidewalk smile at us. To them we look like two girls and a little sister out for a walk on a gorgeous fall day. Unbeknownst to them, we are both hanging on with viselike grips, as letting go could mean picking Patience out from under the wheels of a bus. I'm thinking that the squirrel may have actually thrown himself under the bus in a desperate attempt to flee Patience. And who could blame him?

Since we have to pass the Dairy Delite on the way home anyway, we decide to stop for a root-beer float. Neither of us used our movie-snack money and we're tired of dragging Patience, who is determined to stomp on each and every leaf in the western hemisphere. Allison sits on Patience in a booth while I use a quarter to call my mom and ask her to go across the street and tell Patience's mom that she's with us. I order floats for Allison and me and a small sundae for Patience only because I know I don't have to be around her when the sugar hits her bloodstream.

When I get back to the table with a tray, Allison has magically calmed Patience down. They're talking in quiet voices about school and I actually see Patience listening to Allison's questions and then pausing to think before she blurts out an answer. Amazing! I hand out the ice cream and watch my friend discuss making Halloween masks with Patience as though she were a perfectly be-haved little girl.

After we finish our floats, Allison carries Patience on her back the rest of the way home and answers every one of her questions even though she asks the same one over and over and yells them into her ear. We drop Patience at her house, where her mom thanks us a thousand times and keeps looking anxiously up and down the street for Patience's dad, who's been driving around the neighbour-hood looking for her. I feel sorry for her. A half hour with Patience and I'm exhausted. I can't imagine a lifetime with her.

At my house, Allison and I pick up Elsie and put her on her leash. I grab my jean jacket and we stuff our pock-ets with peanut butter cookies my mom has cooling on the counter. Then we head over to Allison's to pick up her dog. Elvis likes to play with Elsie. He always gets to be boss because he's way older and way bigger, and he doesn't seem to mind that she slobbers all over him. We take them on a long walk through the ravine, where they attack giant piles of leaves and roll around in them. The sun starts to dip in the sky, making the trees in the ravine look like they're on fire. To myself, I decide that autumn is my favourite season, but I know that it would feel a whole lot different if I didn't have Allison here with me.

When it starts to get dark we head back to my house to coerce my mom into pizza. She drives us to Jake's to pick up a large vegetarian with light cheese and extra sauce. We light candles in the dining room and serve the pizza on the good china with linen napkins and crystal goblets, just for laughs — my mom's idea. To make it even funnier, everyone at the table has to speak with an English accent. Halfway through dinner my dad comes home from his squash game and rolls his eyes at us as he steals a piece of pizza. After we load the dishwasher, Allison and I go up to my room and gossip about everyone at school while we play with the dogs until ten, when Allison's mom shows up to take her home.

I curl up with Elsie on my bed and think about how glad I am that today happened. Elsie sticks her paw on my mouth, which is Dog for "Stop thinking and start scratching my belly."

# Chapter 16

When I wanted breasts more than anything in the world, I acted like I didn't care — and they arrived in time for my birthday. When I wanted Allison's friendship back more than anything, I pretended it didn't matter — and we were friends again. Ditto on the Lady Macbeth. I'm trying to behave indifferently. I've banished all thoughts of the role and the play from my head. Is it working? No. No matter how hard I concentrate on other things, I'm back in the castle with a heap of dinner guests, a nervous husband and a dead king every time.

Sunday night I'm a wreck. I toss and turn all night and by half past five I give up. I crawl out my window onto the roof with my comforter wrapped around me and watch my neighbourhood slowly wake up. Lights come on, a car engine starts, the paper boy zooms by on his bike, a dog barks. I shiver and wrap the comforter tighter around me, lie back on the roof and watch the stars disappear as the sky goes from black to indigo.

"Yikes, it's freezing out here."

Elsa is lying next to me wrapped up in an ankle-length multicoloured wool coat. She's wearing a wool cap and suede boots that lace up to her knees.

"What are you wearing? You look like a sherpa."

"You like it?"

"Yeah, but Joseph called. He wants his Technicolor Dreamcoat back."

"Funny. Well, it's all the rage in Morocco."

"I thought it was hot in Morocco."

"Hot days, frigid nights. It's a real wardrobe challenge."

"I can see that. You look a little wardrobe-challenged."

Elsa glares at me. "Moving right along. Now would be a good time to say, 'Hey, Elsa, thanks for all the great advice. Everything worked out just the way you said it would.'"

"I don't know if I got the part yet."

"There are no guarantees in this relationship. I'm not even getting paid for this."

"You're right. Thank you."

"Was that so hard?"

"I'm sorry. I know that this all started as a ploy to fix things with Allison, but everything's different now. Now I want this part more than I ever thought I could. I guess I worry too much. I wonder, though: how many good things can happen to one person? What if you get greedy and want too much, like Ginny and Lady Macbeth? Will the things you get backfire on you?"

Elsa covers her face with her purple wool gloves and shakes her head. "Oy, enough! The important thing is not to get the things you want but to want the things you get. In the meantime, if you want good things to happen to you, make some good things happen to the people around you."

"Like who?" I ask.

Just then we hear a noise from across the street. We get up and peer over the pitch of the roof. Patience is running barefoot across her frosty lawn in pajamas. Under her arm she has a box of Lucky Charms, which is spilling a pastel trail behind her on the lawn. Her mother, a few paces back, is yelling, "Patience, get back here! I mean it!"

Elsa and I look at each other.

"Like her," says Elsa.

The posting outside the Drama room doesn't draw the same crowd as the posting after cheerleader tryouts. Most of us look sullen because that's how we think actors should look. No one is shrieking or jumping up and down or doing cartwheels or the splits.

When I edge my way close enough to the bulletin board to read it, I try to look without looking. My eyes go to Macbeth first: SIMON BECKMAN. Good, that's good. Simon's understudy is someone named Bob Haug (never heard of him). Okay, now let's see here. LADY MACBETH: CLARE FERRON. That's me. That's my name, right? Wow. I did it. I got it.

"Well?" asks Allison from behind me.

"I got it," I say quietly, backing away from the bulletin board. "I got the part. The part of Lady Macbeth will be played by *me*!"

Allison hugs me. I hug her back. I can barely believe it. It's real. I wanted something, I worked hard for it and I got it. Could the world possibly work that way? Wow.

Eric appears at the door of the Drama room and hands out rehearsal schedules to everyone. When I take mine he smiles and says, "Congratulations, Clare, you deserve it."

Allison and I put our heads together and look at the schedule. The play rehearses Mondays, Wednesdays and Fridays after school and half days on Saturdays. We look at each other.

"Well," I say, "there's always Tuesdays and Thursdays."

"I have Track and Field Tuesdays and Thursdays," says Allison.

"Well, Friday nights then," I say.

"I have interpretive dance Fridays."

"Okay then, Sundays."

"Right. Sundays." Allison knows how important this is to me, and she grins and punches me in the shoulder. "C'mon, buck up, you're supposed to suffer for your art. We talked about this, remember?"

"Sure." I smile. But I hadn't really thought it through. The truth is, I hadn't thought about it much past getting the part.

Underneath the rehearsal schedule is a list of phone numbers of everyone involved in the production. Simon's is first on the list. I run my finger over his name. Mine is lower on the list. I imagine Simon attaching this list to his fridge with a magnet, which would mean that my name would be on his fridge. How pathetic is that? Allison's been kissed already and I'm excited about my name being smashed under someone's fridge magnet. Someone who's so far out of my league it isn't even funny.

Allison and I walk to our lockers. I catch myself check-ing around for Ginny until it dawns on me that she isn't going to be around for two whole glorious weeks. We're like a country without its wicked queen. The commoners are laughing and frolicking, carefree and happy, sort of like a Smurf village of eighth graders.

After school I go to my first *Macbeth* rehearsal, which turns out to be more of an orientation. Eric addresses all the actors, understudies, set builders, technical people and wardrobe people camped out in front of him on the carpet. He can't stress enough that we have to do a ton of work in very little time. The play opens on November tenth and runs for two weekends, that's six performances. Eric's high level of enthusiasm is now combined with a drill sergeant's attention to detail that I find a little frightening, but he seems to know what he's doing. After this first meeting we will all split up into our various departments until shortly before the play, when we'll work together again.

Simon is lounging on the carpet with his head propped up on his elbow. He has cleverly mastered a tough-guy/sensitive-type look with just the right amount of brand-new facial hair and a simple gold earring in his left ear balanced by black frame glasses. This is the boy I'm going to be spending hour after hour of my life with for weeks on end? Yikes. He catches me looking at him and nods to me as if he's read my mind. I smile and look away.

After Eric reads us the riot act on missing rehearsals (don't do it) and practising (do it all the time), he lets us go home. My understudy, a ninth grader (ironically), comes over and introduces herself. Her name is Astrid and she seems nice but not entirely comfortable with getting beat out by an eighth grader. I can't really blame her. How would I feel? While I'm talking to her I see Simon walking out the door. Sylvia is waiting just outside for him, and he kisses her and drapes his arm casually over her shoulders as they walk away together, the most perfect couple on Earth.

I walk out the double doors at the end of the hallway and head home. Out on the sports field, Mr. Bianchini is working with the girls' soccer team, doing drills. I stop at the chain-link fence and watch for a minute. He demonstrates a shot on goal, which the goalie misses completely, and then he stands in front of them, talking with his hands and pointing at the goal. Even from all the way back where I'm standing I can tell that most of the girls are in love with him.

I feel nostalgic for the flutter I used to get in my stomach whenever I saw him, but I know that it's not there anymore and it's never coming back. I'm completely over him. I look at him again and remember how Aunt Rusty asked me if I thought he looked happy. If happy means you like what you're doing, I guess he's probably happy.

I put Mr. Bianchini out of my mind and walk home with lines from *Macbeth* swirling around in my head, which makes me feel terribly important in a way I've never really felt before.

# Chapter 17

My life soon becomes a flurry of rehearsals where I change into Lady Macbeth with every cell of my being. Simon is as devoted to his role as I am to mine, so we work well together. Except for a few awkward moments before and after rehearsals, it's easy to be around him because when we're together we're Macbeth and Lady Macbeth. Eric is delighted with us. He cheers and jumps up and down and eggs us on. I honestly never thought I had it in me to work this hard. The wardrobe manager has taken endless embarrassing measurements for my gowns (thank God for the new breasts!), and the sketches she's drawn look rich and glamorous.

At home it's a different story. My mom and dad aren't quite grasping that I'm royalty and continue to treat me like plain old Clare. Somehow, in their silly commoner brains, they believe that I should still be doing chores that only a servant should have to do. It's so degrading, especially when they insist that I pick up dog poo from the back lawn and dispose of it as though I'm some sort of peasant. I explain to them that I've been working hard, rambling through the drafty old castle all day, kicking the help around, but they don't seem to care. They're quick to remind me of the promise I made to be a stand-up dog owner back when I was begging them to let me keep Elsie. As soon as I am queen I will have their heads removed, and then we'll see who's in charge.

After practice, the actors sometimes get together at a diner called Millie's a couple of blocks from the school. Since I'm the only eighth grader in the cast, I feel a bit strange about hanging out with everyone, so for the first week I pretend I have to go right home. But after the second Saturday rehearsal, which is particularly gruelling, Simon asks me to come along.

"Um. I probably shouldn't," I say, pulling my coat on.

"C'mon, if you don't join us it's just me and the three witches. You have to come."

"Well, okay," I say. "Just for a few minutes."

We walk out into the coolish afternoon, the witches trailing behind us. Simon's girlfriend, Sylvia, is nowhere to be seen, which is odd to me because I've never seen them apart outside the Drama room. Simon puts his hands in his pockets and walks next to me on the sidewalk. He chats about the play and I find myself relaxing. He's easy to talk to, and he has a lot to say about things in general, not just *Macbeth*. When we get to the corner where we have to cross the street, he takes my arm lightly and watches for cars as we cross. He tells me that he has three sisters, which explains why he's so comfortable around girls. I tell him I'm an only child but I have a dog, and he asks me all about Elsie. I feel strange, walking next to a ninth-grade boy who is actually listening to me and talking to me like we're friends. It's always felt to me like ninth grade is a different country that's off limits to a mere eighth grader. Eighth grade is a sort of no man's land between childhood and adolescence.

At the diner I follow everyone to a booth in the back. The witches slide in together and Simon sits next to me on the other side. We pull off our coats. The witches' names are Susan, Terry and Susan, which is very confusing. Simon is friendly with the witches and they start chatting away about mostly ninth-grade stuff. I stay pretty quiet. When the waitress comes, everyone orders coffee, so I do, too. She turns our cups right-side up and fills them with the pot in her hand. I put lots of sugar and milk in mine. If my mom knew that I was drinking coffee, she'd kill me. Simon takes a sip of his.

"Disgusting, as usual," he says. "I think I'll get some of that slimy, gelatinous blueberry pie to go with this."

For the most part, the witches act as though I'm not there, but Simon includes me in the conversation as much as he can. When the waitress comes to take our order, Simon asks for blueberry pie and the girls order fries with gravy. I tell the waitress I'm just having coffee, and Simon tells me I have to share his pie with him.

"It's part of the Millie's experience," he says, rolling his eyes.

Terry asks Simon where Sylvia is, and he says she's working at her dad's donut shop.

"She hates it, but she needs the money. She wants to go to France on this exchange program next summer."

"Aren't you going?" asks one of the Susan witches.

"No. I'm terrible at saving money."

"Sylvia and Simon apart?" she says. "Inconceivable."

"Yeah, well, maybe Clare and I will run off and get married. How about it, Clare?"

I blush. "Thanks, but no."

"C'mon. Why not? It's the money, isn't it? Tell me. I can take it. Is it because I'm a penniless actor?"

"No. I already promised I'd run off and marry some-one else."

"Who is he? I'll kill him with my bare hands!" He smacks his fist into the palm of his hand.

I laugh. "You don't know him. He doesn't go to our school."

Simon shrugs and the waitress arrives with his pie, which distracts him. He grabs his fork and digs in. He fills his mouth with pie and looks over at me. There's blueberry pie filling running down his chin.

"You bwoke my hawt," he says with his mouth full.

The witches are delighted with Simon's display. It's obvious that he brings the laughs to these things. They expect him to be funny.

When the waitress slaps the cheque down on our table, I realize with horror that I don't have any money on me. I start to dig through my backpack, feeling terribly lame, pretending to look for money, but Simon grabs the cheque and waves his hand at me.

"The first hit's on me. You get the next one, okay?"

"Okay." I smile, relieved that I didn't have to look like an idiot the first time out with the cast.

We gather up our coats and things, and one of the Susan witches asks what everyone's doing that night. Simon says that he and Sylvia are going to a party; it's the same party the Terry witch is going to. She's dating Steve, who plays the part of Duncan in the play. The other Susan is going to the movies with her girlfriends. I pretend I didn't hear the question because I don't think she was really talking to me anyway.

"*When shall we three meet again?*" asks Terry.

One of the Susan witches says, "Monday, and that's my line."

Everyone says goodbye and we head off in separate directions. As it happens, Simon is going my way and he falls into step next to me.

"Where do you live?" I ask.

"Up there." He points to the hill above us, sprinkled with houses that overlook the river. "How about you?"

"The other way. Down by the ravine, on Birch."

"What's your dad do?" he asks.

"Lawyer," I say with zero enthusiasm.

"Mine, too. How original. He sues companies for a living. You're not going to be a lawyer, are you?"

"No!"

"What do you want to be?" he asks.

"You first. What do you want to be?"

"An actor," he says without even pausing.

"Me, too," I say, surprised at how fast I blurt it out.

Simon looks happy to hear it. "You'll make a great actor," he says.

"So will you," I say.

"*We are yet but young in deed*," he says in his Macbeth voice.

"True enough," I say. "But it's never too early to start thinking about the future."

When we reach the next corner we say goodbye.

"See you Monday, back at the castle." He bows slightly.

We go our separate ways. I cross the street and head toward home. "Actors," I say to myself. "Simon and I want to be actors." I didn't know it until that moment when Simon asked me, but now that I've said it, I couldn't be more sure.

## Chapter 18

On Sunday afternoon I smooth-talk Allison into coming with me to take Patience to one of those places where you paint pottery. I understand that this is a very dicey situation I'm heading into, but I'm willing to take a leap of faith because I'm feeling particularly generous and I'm taking Elsa's words of wisdom to heart.

When we arrive at Patience's door to pick her up, her parents are practically on their knees with gratitude. They shove some money at me to cover their daughter's painting fees and bus fare and, by the looks of it, a little extra to cover breakage and bribery. Patience appears dressed in yet another fetching outfit from the Patience "Fall Collection": purple-and-white-striped tights, the red rubber boots borrowed from the Superman ensemble, a lime-green corduroy jumper and a red plastic fireman's helmet. She's also got her face done up in silvery blue eyeshadow and bright red lipstick.

We walk to the bus stop. Along the way, Patience tells us the story of how she learned to fly a plane yesterday because the pilot wasn't feeling well and asked her to help out. We let her ramble on, asking appropriate questions from time to time, like: "Was it a big plane?"; "Did you land the plane?"; "Did you get a pilot's hat?"

At the bus stop we squish Patience between us on the bench. It feels a lot like having a chimp beside us.

She's all arms and legs and "Look at that!" and "You know what?" and "What's that?" Allison and I take turns fielding questions, but we finally catch on that it isn't really important to answer each question correctly because by the time Patience has asked it, she's already moved on to something else. She smells like peanut butter and dirt. By the time the bus arrives I feel like hanging her by her ankles out the window, but we get on and do the same drill, Patience between us on the seat. I'm so grateful that Allison is being a good sport about all this, even though I'm sure she doesn't quite understand why I'm doing it.

At the pottery painting place, Patience chooses a sea horse to paint, then changes her mind ten times and finally arrives back at the sea horse. The woman who works there is developing a twitch in her right eye, and her voice is a few octaves higher than when we arrived. Patience breaks the first sea horse when she jumps up to grab the purple paint and knocks it onto the floor. The dustpan comes out, and we start again with a new sea horse. Once Patience settles in and focuses on painting, I can see that she is really enjoying herself. She smiles at us and concentrates fiercely on getting the eyes on the sea horse right. She hums a little song. Allison and I paint big mugs. I make one for her and she makes one for me, which is tough to do because we're keeping one eye on Patience at all times.

When Patience discovers she can't take her sea horse home today because it has to be fired, she throws a fit and scratches the woman's arm, drawing blood. We apologize and finally drag Patience out of there screaming, much to the relief of the mommies, the employees and the normal kids.

On the bus ride home, Allison and I are running out of steam and watch helplessly as Patience asks a woman why she's so fat and a balding man what happened to his hair. She also asks the bus driver where he got his uniform and how much money he makes.

We deposit Patience on her doorstep. Her parents seem shocked to see us all back in one piece without bandages or the police. We quickly say goodbye and dash across the street to my house, locking the door behind us and collapsing in a heap. I feel as though we've just delivered a load of plutonium. My mom has veggie burgers for us, with chocolate-chip cookies for dessert. She understands that what we just did was the Mount Everest of child care, and she's impressed. I'm not sure she understands that even though Patience can make you want to drop her off a cliff, she also has a way of getting under your skin. There's something about her, even with all her craziness, that is quite loveable. I wouldn't want a steady diet of her, but she does get to me. Maybe it's because I can relate to her being different from all the other kids.

After we finish the burgers, Allison and I go to my room and catch up. We sprawl on my bed, and Elsie jumps up to join us. Between the play and Allison's track stuff, we always have a lot to talk about. I tell Allison all about Simon. She already knows him because he's friends with Troy (who has reinstated himself in Allison's life as a "friend" for now). Allison also knows Sylvia, and she tells me that she's a really nice person, which is not exactly what I want to hear. I'd rather hear that she's a monster. I'm looking for even the slightest possibility that Simon and Sylvia's relationship could end, but even if it did, that doesn't mean he'd be interested in me. Anyway, Allison says that they'll probably be together forever.

"Forever is a long time," I say. "How can you possibly know at fourteen who you want to spend your life with? Who do they think they are, Romeo and Juliet?"

"My parents met when they were fourteen."

"They did?"

"Yeah. My dad saved my mom from drowning."

"You're kidding!"

"Nope."

"Well, when someone saves your life, spending the rest of it with them is the least you can do."

Allison laughs. "You make it sound so romantic."

Allison and I finally talk about the fact that Ginny is coming back to school the next morning. It's been a blissful two weeks, but I know Allison is dreading having to face Ginny. I'm sure that two weeks alone has given Ginny lots of time to cool off, but an ousted queen has trouble holding her head up after a fall from grace, and she'll want to point the finger at someone — like me, for instance. The truth is, I'm not really afraid. I have faith in my friendship with Allison and I know that she'll support me. Besides, even Eddie, the janitor at our school, knows the whole story. You'd have to be living in a cave on Mars with your fingers in your ears not to have heard it.

"You know, I'm not really even angry at Ginny," says Allison, scratching Elsie's belly.

"You're a bigger person than I am. What if her plan had worked?"

"It didn't. You were there to save me. The whole thing taught me a lesson about trust. I guess I thought I was a better judge of character than I am. I should have trusted you when you warned me about her."

"Don't worry. Even I underestimated what Ginny was capable of when she's at her most evil. She makes Cruella De Vil look like a girl scout."

"The other night I was looking at Troy's yearbook from last year, and do you know how many times Ginny appears in it?"

"Twenty-seven."

"That's right! And she was only in seventh grade!"

"Did you count the times that I appear?"

Allison starts to laugh. "Yes, as a matter of fact I did."

"How many?" I ask as if I don't know.

"Once. But I gave you another half because I recognized you from behind in one of the pictures of Ginny at the track meet."

I sock her in the head with my Spider-Man pillow.

Elsie and I walk Allison home under a moon so big and golden it looks like it's right out of a fairy tale. Thanksgiving is in the air. Primitive construction-paper turkeys decorate the windows of the houses we pass, and scarecrows and baskets of pumpkins and gourds and coloured corn sit on people's front porches. I'm glad that Thanksgiving falls before Halloween in Canada. The Americans group it together with Christmas and call the whole thing "The Holiday Season." Judging by all the TV commercials, which have already started appearing on the American channels, I think they should call it "Shopping Season."

Every year I tell my mom that I don't want to do Thanksgiving, because I think it's hypocritical to celebrate the exploitation of the Native peoples, but then I get swept up in the pumpkin pie and the sweet potatoes with marshmallows and the turkey and end up making my mom write a cheque to the First Nations Education Fund in lieu of a boycott. It was a lot easier to say we should skip it when my mom was a lawyer and Thanksgiving came in a big takeout box from the supermarket. Now it throws her into high gear in the kitchen. She keeps the TV on the food channel every waking hour and food magazines cover every available surface; she special-orders fresh organic cranberries and drives all the way to Little Italy for the chestnuts.

Allison's family has a vegetarian Thanksgiving, which sounds fine on paper, but I just can't imagine tofu turkey. I make sure my mom gets our turkey from a farm where the turkeys roam freely and live full turkey lives, a sort of Club Med for turkeys until someone chops their heads off.

The smell of woodsmoke curls up our noses as we crunch the dry leaves under our feet. Elsie tugs at the leash, sniffing imaginary dogs all the way to Allison's house.

# Chapter 19

*"Something wicked this way comes."*
SECOND WITCH

Allison is the first person to see the graffiti on Ginny's locker. I am just commenting on the unmistakeable shift in the air that morning when Allison grabs my arm. I spin around and come face to face with the word **THIEF** jaggedly written across Ginny's locker. It looks suspiciously like the same red lipstick that the graffiti on the memo about cell phones was written in. Allison and I freeze, not sure what to do next, but it doesn't matter anyway. Ginny is approaching from the end of the hallway, her noticeably smaller entourage hanging on her every word. When she sees Allison and me standing by her locker, she seems to miss a beat, then picks up again where she left off until she sees her locker.

"It's amazing what petty little games people will resort to when they have no lives," says Ginny, looking directly at me.

"I didn't do it," I say. "Would I be standing here if I did?"

Ginny smears her finger through the "T" and looks at it. "You're right. This is lipstick. You wouldn't even know where to get something like this. Well, at least I know I was missed."

And then I hear someone behind me say in a soft voice that I barely hear, "Don't flatter yourself."

I look around. I'm sure I didn't imagine it, but no one standing there could possibly have said it. These girls are all Ginny's friends. Then a girl named Darla, Ginny's number one lady-in-waiting, meets my eyes. Her face is expressionless, but she's looking right at me and her lips are the same colour as the lipstick on the locker. I touch Allison on the shoulder and signal for her to follow me. When we're at my locker and out of Ginny's earshot, I tell her what I saw.

"Darla, a traitor? She's like Ginny's personal assistant."

"Yeah, it's a bit bizarre all right. But what if she's like one of those junior executives who gets the inside track from the boss and then steals her job?"

Allison shrugs. "I suppose it's possible, but how's she going to get rid of Ginny?"

"She'll kill her and make it look like an accident or suicide or something like that."

"Slow down, Nancy Drew. I think you're getting a little ahead of yourself."

We head off to our homerooms, but thoughts of murder and deceit are dancing in my head for most of homeroom and into my first class. I'm fascinated at the prospect of an insider overthrowing Ginny's dictatorship.

As luck would have it, today is Track-and-Field day. I have to admit that since I've become a drama queen the whole track-and-field thing just doesn't excite me much.

I like the running but I rarely muster up any team spirit. Allison, on the other hand, is like an eager filly. She's definitely going to be the star of the track team this year, leaving all of us, including Ginny, in her dust. I couldn't be happier for her, especially now that I know it's going to drive Ginny crazy.

We gather out near the track in our shorts, our arms and legs covered in goosebumps. This might be one of the last outdoor classes. Soon we'll move into the gymnasium for the winter, where everything smells like old sweat and our sneakers make that unbearable high-pitched squeak when we run.

Mr. Bianchini, who usually embraces the cold with a sort of hivey, hovey Nordic spirit, seems to be shivering today. He looks a little pale, and he's got the hood of his sweatshirt pulled up over his head and his hands stuffed into the pockets. Ginny dances on the spot, eager to get going. It's probably because she spent the last two weeks lounging on her sofa, eating potato chips and planning her comeback. As soon as Mr. Bianchini blows his whistle and sends us on our way around the track, Ginny takes off like a shot and passes everyone. Allison rolls her eyes and we jog around the track together, taking our time. Allison doesn't run like the wind unless someone's timing her.

Halfway around the track I notice Mr. Bianchini is walking away and heading toward the playground. He usually watches us run, taking notes and yelling encouraging things at us, but today he looks like some-one who's completely lost interest. He sits down on a swing and drags his feet through the sand. He glances at us from time to time, but mostly he just stares down at the sand. I suddenly realize who's responsible for this: Aunt Rusty! She must have broken up with him. No wonder he's walking around like a wounded dog. I'm so busy feeling sorry for Mr. Bianchini that I don't notice Ginny Germain writhing on the sidelines, holding her ankle. Allison runs over to her and I trail behind, turn-ing to see if Mr. Bianchini has snapped out of his daze. He's on his feet, running.

"Ow! Ow! I think it's broken," moans Ginny.

Mr. Bianchini kneels next to her and feels for broken bones. "It's just a pull. You shouldn't have been running so fast. It's cold out, and you're out of shape. It's a warm-up run, not a hundred-metre dash."

"We'll see about that." She glares at Mr. Bianchini. "I'm going to see the nurse." Ginny hobbles off the field, leaning on a girl who is probably too afraid of Ginny not to help her. We watch as Ginny scolds the girl for walk-ing too fast.

Mr. Bianchini looks totally despondent and tells us that's it for the day, we can go. I feel awful for him, but I think I'm the last person who should say something.

I head directly for the pay phone outside the gym, telling Allison I'll meet her in the girls' locker room in a minute. I drop in a quarter and dial Aunt Rusty's number. I get the answering machine, but that means nothing. She rarely answers her phone. I listen to the outgoing message.

"Hey, it's Rusty. If this is Tish, I meant the red one, not the purple one, and I'll see you at six. Everyone else: you know what to do. Don't forget to wait for the beep."

"Aunt Rusty, it's Clare. Pick up the phone. It's an emergency."

Aunt Rusty picks up. "Clare? Are you okay?"

"Yeah, I just wanted you to answer the phone. Did you, by any chance, break up with Mr. Bianchini?"

"He told you?!"

"No. He didn't have to. He's wandering around the schoolyard like a suicidal zombie."

"He seemed fine when I told him."

"Well, maybe he's had some time to think about it."

"Wow. Maybe I underestimated his feelings for me."

"Ya *think?*" I say sarcastically.

"Hey, don't get mad at me. I thought you hated that we were dating."

"I dunno. I guess I got used to it. Anyway, I gotta go. I just thought you should know that he's pretty sad and maybe you should call him later."

"Okay, okay. I will."

I hang up the phone and stand there for a minute. Poor Mr. Bianchini. I think it's important that I take some responsibility for what he's going through. After all, he and

Aunt Rusty never would have met if I hadn't asked Aunt Rusty to come watch me race at the school track meet. On the other hand, I can't always be taking responsibility for other people's mistakes, and that's what Aunt Rusty and Mr. Bianchini were — a mistake.

At the end of the hallway I see Ginny Germain emerging from the nurse's office. I guess the nurse couldn't find any broken bones either. She hobbles down the hallway toward me. Maybe it's my imagination, but I suddenly feel a chilly draft prickle my skin. I shiver and duck into the girls' locker room before she sees me.

# Chapter 20

*"If good, why do I yield to that suggestion*
*Whose horrid image doth unfix my hair*
*And make my seated heart knock at my ribs ..."*
MACBETH

Simon takes a sip of his coffee and continues to explain to me how the play *Macbeth* imitates real life. "You see, though, don't you? It's all about power. Women are the powerful ones. Macbeth would have crawled up the ladder, slow and steady, if Lady Macbeth hadn't kicked him into a higher gear, right?"

"Right," I say, watching the way his hands move. His long thin fingers have a graceful way of arching, and he has a habit of opening his palms when he finishes making a point as though he wants you to see that he's being honest, nothing up his sleeve. He takes a bite of congealing blueberry pie from the plate sitting between us on the Formica table. I lost interest in it a long time ago because it's gross.

I look around. "Why do we come here?" I ask.

"What do you mean?"

"I mean, why do we come here? The coffee's awful, the pie is disgusting, the burgers are greasy and the service is terrible."

Simon looks around. "I guess it's the ambience."

"Yeah, that's gotta be it," I say, letting my eyes drift over the waitress reading a spy novel at the counter and the row of empty vinyl booths behind us.

"Hey, and don't forget the music," he says, pointing his finger to the ceiling. He does a little dance in his seat.

"Yeah. I love that. They play it at my dentist's."

There is something about this place, though. It feels a whole lot more grown-up than the Dairy Delite, although I'd kill for a root-beer float right now. This place has become our clubhouse. After every rehearsal you can find some of us here. It's like *Cheers* without the beer. Eric even comes sometimes. One time he brought his wife, Janice. She's a nurse, which explains the surgery scrubs Eric is always wearing. She's quiet and she looks like the female version of him.

Sometimes, like tonight, it's just Simon and me, which is great. I've become so comfortable with Simon that I can talk about almost anything. He's taken it upon himself to become a sort of big brother to me, which is probably the best I can hope for.

I run my finger through the dust on the leaf of a plastic plant in the window. "What are you and Sylvia doing for Thanksgiving?" I ask, wiping my finger on my jeans.

"Well, Sylvia's dad is a great cook. He's Italian and he does this amazing Italian spread, nothing like the stuff we eat. Thanksgiving is a huge celebration for Sylvia's family because they never had it in Italy, so he reinvented it. It's one of the only days he closes the donut shop."

"So you eat at Sylvia's."

"Here's what I do. My mom would get really bent out of shape if I missed Thanksgiving at our house, but she serves the meal in the afternoon. It's all white linens and the good china and polished silver and classical music and candlesticks. You know, your basic nightmare. Sylvia's family eats late, so I duck out of my family's dinner after dessert and head over to Sylvia's where it's loud music and laughing and dancing and great food. In other words, fun."

"You dog."

"I know," he grins. "Isn't it great?"

"Don't you have to help clean up at your house?"

"I've got three sisters, remember?"

"You double dog!"

He laughs. "You are so jealous."

"Am not," I say, but I really am. I'm starting to understand the bond between Simon and Sylvia. Her family has become his family and they probably love him to death. Simon has told me more than once that his mom doesn't think he should have a girlfriend at his age, but I'm sure Sylvia's family thinks it's just fine.

"Hey," says Simon, "you wanna come?"

"Where?"

"To Sylvia's. Her parents wouldn't care one bit. They'd love you. You gotta be careful of her dad, though. He squeezes your head really hard between his monster hands and says, 'You too skinny! Eat! Eat!'"

"Thanks. It really sounds great but I've got dinner at my house. My mom is an obsessive cook and I'm an only child. I think I'd be missed."

Simon shrugs and takes a sip of sludge.

"Can I ask you a personal question?"

"Absolutely not."

"C'mon," I say.

"Just kidding. Of course you can, anything. But I must warn you, I'm a pathological liar."

I forge ahead. "Do you remember the first time you kissed Sylvia?"

"Absolutely. Third grade, back of the school bus, it was spectacular."

"No, I mean really *kissed* her."

"Oh, well, Sylvia and I weren't always together, you know. We had a fight that lasted from the end of fourth grade to the end of seventh grade."

"What about?" I ask.

"I think she decided I was icky and she didn't want my boy germs anywhere near her. But by eighth grade she started really liking my germs."

"And?"

"And what?"

"The kiss."

"Oh right, the kiss. I believe it was the eighth-grade dance. We were hiding out under the bleachers and I just grabbed her and kissed her like they do on TV. That was the first time I got wobbly kissing her, and when I opened my eyes and looked at Sylvia, I knew it was the same for her."

"Wow," I say. "I'm getting chills."

"How about you?" he asks.

I blush. "Well, it hasn't exactly happened yet."

"The kiss or the wobbly part?"

I play with my coffee spoon. "Um … the kiss."

"Why not? Playing hard to get?"

"No. Boys don't like me."

"I like you."

"I know but … not like that."

"Well, the guys at school, they're mostly idiots. You know that, don't you?"

"Sure." I look down at the table.

"Don't worry, Clare. The less you fit in, the better off you are."

I look up at him. "You think so?"

"I know so," he says, winking at me. "Now let's get the cheque and get out of this dump."

We pay up and walk out into the chilly, early evening air. The days are getting shorter and shorter and it's already dark as midnight. I pull on my coat and my furry aviator's cap with the earflaps, and we both hoist our backpacks onto our shoulders. Simon stuffs his hands into the pockets of his navy peacoat and shivers. We walk along in silence together. Every few steps Simon shoves me, and then I shove him back, until we reach the corner where we say goodbye and go off in our separate directions.

When I arrive home, my mom is in the kitchen. She looks at the clock on the stove as I plunk my backpack on a kitchen chair.

"It's getting late," she says. "I was worried. Where were you?"

"Oh, you know, same old thing, I was doing shots at

Duke's bar and I don't like to come home till I'm good and drunk."

She ignores me. "Were you at that diner again? You didn't ruin your appetite, did you?"

"Not much chance of that. The food is inedible."

I sit on the floor and wrestle with Elsie. My mom steps over me, pulls a loaf of garlic bread out of the oven and puts it in a wicker basket. Then she drains a pot of linguine into the sink. The steam rises up and coats the window in front of her. Elsie pulls at my old torn-up slipper, now a chew toy, coaxing me to play tug-of-war with her.

"Mom, do you think we could invite Patience and her mom and dad for Thanksgiving?"

"Sure. If you want to. Don't you think they're already going somewhere?"

"No. I bet they're not. No one in their right mind would have Patience in their home for that long."

"So we're out of our minds, is that it?"

"Yeah. Careful with the good dishes. I'd use paper plates if I were you."

"That will be lovely," says my mom, who lives for beautiful table settings.

"Also, you should probably skip the candles, and knives would be a mistake, too."

"I'll bear that in mind. Speaking of which, can you set the table, honey? Dinner's ready."

I struggle to my feet and drag Elsie through the kitchen by the slipper, which she refuses to let go of.

"We have insurance though, right, Mom?"

# Chapter 21

"It had been as a gap in our great feast,
And all-thing unbecoming."
LADY MACBETH

Thanksgiving day is clear and crisp and perfect. I take Elsie for a walk over to Allison's house, inhaling the smell of roasting turkeys and baking pumpkin pies from every house along the way. Elsie's plan is to drop in on every house for a little snack, and I have to keep tugging her back onto the sidewalk. The fabulous smells stop at Allison's house, where an anemic, greyish, soy turkey, which couldn't look less like a turkey, sits on the kitchen counter. Allison's mom is peeling potatoes at the table. I say "hi" and give her the pumpkin bread my mom sent over. It's wrapped in tissue printed with autumn leaves and tied with orange raffia. My mom loves a motif.

Elsie and Elvis crash into each other like old friends reunited, and we take them out for a walk together. Elsie is slowly catching up to Elvis in size, but he can still pin her in a second. I sometimes think she lets him because he needs to be the boss. In a couple of months they'll be almost the same size and then Elsie's going to have to win the odd round.

As we head down into the ravine, Allison and I catch each other up on our lives because we're both so busy these days that we barely have time to talk on the phone, let alone see each other. I tell her my friendship with Simon is progressing, and I know that I don't have to tell her I think he's pretty special. I don't feel like moaning on about unrequited love. I'm already well on my way to becoming the patron saint of lost causes. For Troy and Allison it's the other way around. She explains the complicated dynamics to me.

"He calls me all the time and we talk, and then the talk always gets around to why I won't be his girlfriend. Besides being strictly verboten by my parents, which I don't mention, I always tell him that I'm not ready for a boyfriend right now. I don't really even want to be someone's girlfriend. It's such an icky term. It implies that you're a possession of theirs, like a car or a stereo."

"Or a set of golf clubs," I offer.

Allison looks confused. "Whatever ... anyways, sometimes he comes by and pretends he was just in the neighbourhood. My mom always gives him cookies or a sandwich, like he's a stray dog or something. He sits there at the kitchen table, eating and looking at me, and then he leaves. It's very uncomfortable."

"It's got to be a little bit nice, though. I mean, being pursued like that?"

Allison shrugs. "Sure, I guess. But sometimes I wonder if he's just doing that thing that boys do where the more you tell them no, the more they chase you. I don't get why he's not chasing some Barbie-doll cheerleader type."

"Maybe because there's a million of them around and there's only one of you."

"Who knows?" she says, ignoring the compliment.

I can see Elsie's tail wagging a few yards in front of us, but Elvis seems to have disappeared. Allison whistles for him, and we hear him crashing through the trees. He emerges from the underbrush with burrs and leaves tangled in his fur. We hike out of the ravine and say goodbye in front of Allison's house. Elsie and I jog home together, Elsie in the lead because she senses that there's going to be food at the other end. Her first Thanksgiving and she's already got the hang of it.

Aunt Rusty's convertible is parked at the curb outside my house. For a moment I entertain the possibility that Mr. Bianchini could be inside my house, but I decide that life probably doesn't work that way. I remember having a hissy fit at the idea that he might come to my birthday party last summer (he didn't), and now that I'm coming from a much more mature place and wouldn't mind having him here, it's out of the question. I am always glad to see Aunt Rusty, though.

I pull open the front door and the smell of roasting turkey smacks me in the face. The kitchen is warm and cozy, and Aunt Rusty is sitting on a bar stool with a glass of wine, watching my mom cook. Elsie and I give her a cuddly hello, and I pull up a bar stool next to her. She's wearing a nice black dress with combat boots, and she has yellow paint on her right knee.

"Your mom says you're rehearsing *Macbeth* day and night."

"Yup," I say, sticking my finger in a bowl of mashed sweet potatoes and licking it.

"Well, God knows I never hear from you anymore, unless you count boyfriend advice."

I look at my mom, who's got the oven open, basting a turkey the size of a Buick. She doesn't seem to be listening. "Did you call him?" I whisper.

"Yes, I called him. He wasn't hanging from the chandelier or anything like that, but it did sound like he'd been doing some thinking."

"And?" I ask impatiently.

"And nothing. I told him to call me if he wants to talk. I left it at that."

"Okay." I exhale slowly.

"Sheesh, Clare, you wanna take it down a couple of notches? You're acting a little intense for a thirteen-year-old."

"Now I'm a thirteen-year-old? This from a woman who asked me to break up with her boyfriend for her?"

My mom looks up from her turkey, baster in hand. "You did what?"

"Nothing," Aunt Rusty says, punching me in the arm. She leans over the counter, reaches for the wine bottle and refills her glass.

"Will you two light the candles in the dining room? And Clare, will you tell your dad to start a fire? It's going to be cold tonight."

Aunt Rusty and I get up from our bar stools and head into the dining room. On the way past the staircase I yell, "Dad, Mom wants you to light a fire!"

The dining room table looks like Martha Stewart herself stopped by. There is a tiny pumpkin at each place setting with a place card wedged into it. I wonder how long it will take for Patience to start hurling those across the room. I quickly rearrange the little pumpkins so that Patience is next to me instead of between her parents. Then I remove the knife from her place. Aunt Rusty rifles through the drawers of the buffet, looking for matches, until my mom walks in and hands her a large automatic fireplace lighter.

"Oh, good, a flame-thrower, thanks," she says, taking it from her.

Aunt Rusty starts lighting the candles, which match the table linens, the gigantic flower arrangement and the autumn wreath perfectly. My dad comes down the stairs, talking on the phone, and goes out the front door to the woodpile. I can hear him still talking as he grabs a stack of wood and comes back in. We'll be lucky if he hangs up to eat.

My mom tells us to open some more wine and makes a point of noticing that Aunt Rusty already drank most of the first bottle. Aunt Rusty ignores her, and I'm grateful because all it takes is one "What do you mean by that?" and they're off.

My aunt and I get back on our bar stools and start singing along to "Moondance" by Van Morrison, which is my mom's favourite cooking music. We sing into the pepper mill cheek to cheek as if we're Van Morrison's backup singers. My mom smiles at us, takes a container of home-made cranberry sauce out of the fridge and pours it into a crystal bowl. I dip my finger into it and my mom gives me a look. I lick it off my finger. It's tart and spicy and delicious, a thousand times better than the stuff with the can imprint on it that she used to serve with the takeout turkey when she was a lawyer.

My mom opens the oven and bastes the turkey again. Van starts in on "Crazy Love." Just as my mom shuts the oven door we hear the horrible screech of tires outside, followed by the bang you always wait for after the screech. We run to the front door. A woman is crouching in front of her car. She stands up with her hand over her mouth and looks around at us.

"Call an ambulance!" she screams. "Someone call an ambulance!"

# Chapter 22

I sit in the uncomfortable turquoise-vinyl hospital chair with my knees drawn up to my chin and my arms wrapped around my shins. I've been sitting this way for three hours. Patience barely makes a lump under the hospital sheets as her tiny body lies there with tubes stuck into every available inch. Her little purple cast lies on top of the sheets. She looks like a cartoon character who's been flattened by a bulldozer. I expect her to have cartoon Xs on her eyes. The beeping and sucking sounds of the various machines, combined with all the regular hospital coming and going sounds, have become comforting to me because I know they're all part of the big machine that could save Patience.

Once the doctor told everyone that there was nothing we could do but wait, my parents and Aunt Rusty went home and Patience's mom and dad went to the cafeteria for a cup of tea, but I couldn't move. My mom said she'd be back with turkey sandwiches for me.

I'm trying to psychically get inside Patience's brain to tell her to wake up. I'm sending her positive energy and promising her all sorts of good things if she will just wake up. I try to stay optimistic, but I feel horribly guilty because Patience was running across the street to my house when the woman hit her. In other words, none of this would have happened if I hadn't invited

Patience for Thanksgiving. It's not the woman's fault. She couldn't have stopped in time. She wasn't even going that fast. She was looking at house numbers, trying to find her friend's house, when Patience flew out in front of her. She said that at first she thought it was just a bird. That was probably because Patience was wearing an Indian head-dress with lots of feathers.

A nurse comes in every half hour to check the machines and take Patience's blood pressure. She smiles at me and I search her face for some answers, but she doesn't tell me anything. She'd make a great poker player. After another hour passes, my mom comes back with a turkey sandwich and some orange juice. I drink the juice and pick at the sandwich, never once taking my eyes off Patience, who hasn't moved in four hours. My mom puts her arm across my shoulders and we sit there together. The nurses throw us out when visiting hours end, and we walk to the car silently. When we get home my mom has magically made Thanksgiving disappear as though it never happened.

I call Allison and tell her about the accident. She starts to cry when I tell her about Patience in her little bed, not moving. I know she understands. It's like a hummingbird suddenly stopping in midflight. Elsie won't let me out of her sight, and when I get into bed she curls up next to me. I try to put the thought of Patience alone in the hospital, at-tached to those big machines, out of my mind, but I can't.

The next morning I can hear my mom on the phone downstairs, talking to Patience's mom. I run downstairs and I can tell by my mom's face that Patience is going to be okay. Apparently she woke up at midnight and is already driving the nurses nuts. My mom won't let me skip school to go to the hospital, but she says I can go right after school. I may as well have skipped for all the attention I give to my classes. After school I take the bus to the pottery-painting place, where I pick up the painted sea horse and the mugs Allison and I painted. I can't believe it took me this long to come back for this stuff, but I guess I was thinking about the play. The woman who works there remembers Patience as if it were yesterday. I get back on the bus and look out the window, laughing as I remember the day Patience chased the bus in her superhero costume.

I get off at the hospital. Patience is sitting up in her bed and there's now a cast on her right leg, which is broken in four places. The machines are all gone. She has a bandage on her forehead and a splint on her right index finger. Other than that, she looks okay. I take the sea horse out of the bag and put it on the bedside table facing her. She looks at it and smiles at me.

"Thanks," she says quietly. "I got run over."

"I know," I say. "But you'll be okay."

"Will you stay and talk to me?" she asks sleepily.

"Sure," I say.

I pull up a chair next to the bed. I talk to her about whatever I can think of: winter, school, animals, Christmas, candy, comic books, movies, trees.

The next day I talk about airplanes, music, colours, movie stars, books, spiders. The day after that I talk about planets, dinosaurs, zoos, rockets, toys. Elsa even shows up to keep me company and sits across the bed from me in her own chair. We watch Patience together. Elsa gives me some more things to talk about: Halloween, summer, hair, ice cream and money. Allison drops by with a plant for Patience and some banana muffins for me. On the fourth day I begin to run out of things to talk about so I read *Macbeth* to her till she complains. Then I switch over to comic books.

On the fifth day I'm curled up in my chair, watching Patience sleep with her arm wrapped around a stuffed penguin, when Simon walks through the door of her hospital room. I've missed three *Macbeth* rehearsals, which is bad. I think he's here to talk about that, but he pulls up a chair next to mine and sits down. He hands me a little paper bag.

"Gummi bears," he says.

"Thanks. How did you find me?" I ask.

"Your mom. I called your house." He looks at Patience. "Is she okay?"

I nod. "She will be. She hit her head pretty hard so they had to keep her here a while, but the doctor says she might be able to go home tomorrow."

"We miss you," he says, turning to me.

I'm so happy he put it that way instead of, "You better not miss any more rehearsals."

"I miss you, too," I say.

We sit there for a minute, watching Patience, who looks like an angel when she's asleep.

"Well, I better get going," he says.

"Okay."

Simon faces me, and I think he's going to tell me something really serious, but he doesn't. Instead he leans in and kisses me softly on the lips. Not a friendly peck, a real kiss. When he pulls away, he's smiling a little. He gets up out of the chair.

"See you at rehearsal," he says.

"Sure." I wave as he walks out the door.

I watch him walk by the big glass windows and disappear.

Wow. My first kiss. In a hospital, wearing the same clothes I've worn for the last four days, greasy hair, dry lips, a bag of gummi bears in my hand, and there it is, right out of the blue. I notice that Patience is watching me.

"Who was that boy?" she asks.

"A friend from school," I say.

"Is he your boyfriend?"

"No."

"Then why was he kissing you?"

"Because," I say.

"Because why?"

"Because I wanted him to."

"Can I have some chocolate pudding?"

"Sure."

Patience is released from the hospital the next morning. She throws a fit in her wheelchair when she finds out she won't be riding home in an ambulance. I'm not there, but her mom tells me about it and I'm sure it was spectacular. She has to stay in bed for a while, and she won't be walking for a month. Fortunately the pain medication should keep her calm. In a week or so, when she's feeling better, a physical therapist will visit her every day. I don't think the doctors understand that Patience is made of rubber and it would take more than getting hit by a car to keep her down.

As for me, I'm feeling much better knowing that Patience is going to be okay ... for now.

# Chapter 23

> *"Foul whisp'rings are abroad. Unnatural deeds*
> *Do breed unnatural troubles."*
> DOCTOR

I go back to my life and rehearsals for *Macbeth*. Eric lets me have it for missing three rehearsals. Apparently *I* would have to be the one hit by a car for it to count as a good excuse. When I finally get onstage I'm eager to prove to Eric how quickly I can get back on track, but I soon realize that he was right. Missing rehearsals is not a good idea. I barely looked at the play while Patience was in the hospital, and the dress rehearsal is right around the corner. We begin with Act 5, Scene 1, the scene where Lady Macbeth goes insane from all the guilt. I start out fine:

> *"Out, damned spot. Out, I say. One. Two.*
> *Why, then 'tis time to do't. Hell is murky ..."*

I freeze. My heart starts to pound. I have no idea what's next.

Astrid, my understudy, prompts me from backstage. *"Fie, my lord, fie! a soldier ..."*

*"Fie, my lord, fie! a soldier and afeard?"* I freeze again. My mind is a complete blank.

Astrid prompts me again. "*What need we fear who knows it ...*"

"*What need we fear who knows it ...*" I don't know what's next. I can see Simon out of the corner of my eye willing me to continue. The Doctor and the Gentlewoman on-stage with me exchange glances. Eric, sitting in a seat a few rows back from the stage, shakes his head. I imagine all the seats full of people, shaking their heads.

Astrid tries again. "*When none can call our power to account?*"

I turn on Astrid, wanting to kill her. I realize that she's not reading from the book. She's memorized it. She knows the part better than I do. She looks the part more than I do. She's waiting, enjoying this. Everybody's waiting. All the actors who have already learned their lines are waiting for me. My cheeks are on fire. I turn back to Eric.

"I'm sorry, I guess I just ..."

"Clare, are you okay?" he asks.

I dash down the stairs and out the door. Tears roll down my cheeks. I push open the heavy exit doors and sit on the cold concrete steps, shivering, my face in my hands. What was I thinking? An actor? On a stage? I'm terrified. Maybe I stayed in that hospital with Patience because of the little voice inside me that kept saying, "You're no actor, you're a fake."

I hear the door open and shut behind me. I'm sort of expecting Elsa, but it's Simon who sits down next to me.

"Sheesh, what a drama queen," he says.

"I can't do it. I suck."

"You don't suck. You froze. Actors do it all the time."

I look up at Simon. "If I'm freezing now, what will I be like with a full house?"

"It doesn't work like that. The audience inspires you, they spur you on. You forget to be scared. You'll see."

"Really?"

"Sure. Anyway, it's not about the lines. Anyone can memorize the lines. It's about the acting, and you need talent for that and you've got that talent. You just have to work harder than you've ever worked on anything in your life." Simon stands up and puts out his hand. "C'mon back in or you'll freeze for real."

I wipe my tears on my sleeve and take his hand.

We go back into the Drama room. Eric has moved everyone on to the next scene. He walks over to me.

"Are you ready to try again?" he asks kindly.

I nod.

"Are you ready to take this seriously?" he asks, less kindly.

I thrust my chin out. "Yes."

"Okay, now get up there and act like you mean it."

So I do. And it works. I'm still shaky, but I promise myself that I will work every waking moment on this from now on. I will be ready. I won't disappoint these people and I won't listen to the stupid little voice.

I'm grateful to Simon for talking me out of my fears. We don't ever talk about the kiss, but we treat each other a tiny bit differently now. Not like there's this "thing" between us, but like we know each other a little bit better. Of course, Allison has heard all the minute details of the event and agrees that it was a full-on, all-out kiss. She says she's really happy that my first kiss happened the way it did. I am, too, even though I'd always imagined I'd be wearing an evening gown or at least a party dress and there would be soft lighting and background music and my hair would be combed. But a kiss is a kiss and I have a feeling that when I look back on this one, it might be the best ever.

## Chapter 24

While I was caught up in all the drama over Patience (not to mention the drama over Drama), I missed Ginny Germain's latest misadventure. The next morning at school, Allison shows me a photocopy of a list written in Ginny's handwriting, which has been passed around the whole school. Somehow a page of doodlings from Ginny's notebook was stolen and mysteriously photo-copied and distributed. The page is a very insulting list of the best- and worst-dressed students in the school, starting with Ginny at the top of the best-dressed col-umn and ending with Allison and me at the bottom of the worst-dressed column, with "Bag Ladies" in brackets behind our names. Above our names are the names of several eighth- and ninth-grade girls and boys with com-ments after each one like "His mother still dresses him" and "Wake up, the 80s are over." Needless to say, the list fell into many of the wrong hands. As if that weren't bad enough, apparently the list made it to the principal's office and there has been talk of school uniforms! If that ever happens, Ginny will be tarred and feathered and left tied to the flagpole in front of the school.

Allison and I look at each other and start to laugh. If there is such a thing as karma, I think Ginny's is finally catching up with her. We both agree that it looks sus-piciously like Darla's handiwork. As Ginny's personal assistant, she would have access to her books. If I were Ginny, I would hire a bodyguard immediately.

At the next *Macbeth* rehearsal I'm desperate to prove my commitment to the part. I know the day's lines forward and backward and inside out. Eric is delighted.

The sets are starting to come together and it's a lot more fun to be on stage. The basic set is pretty minimal. It's the interior of the castle, which can quickly be switched to look like the outdoors, with bare trees that the stagehands put into drilled holes on the stage floor to represent Birnam Wood.

> *"Macbeth shall never vanquished be until*
> *Great Birnam Wood to high Dunsinane Hill*
> *Shall come against him."*

A huge dining-room table and chairs will be carried in and a big metal chandelier with real burning candles lowered for the feast at Macbeth's castle. The colours of the set are gloomy greys and black because the play was written that way. There isn't one sunny scene in *Macbeth*. It's all moody and overcast.

The dress I will wear for most of the play is almost finished. It's scarlet satin, rather low-cut in the front (yikes!), and it falls to the floor with a bit of a train at the back. The sleeves are very long, and they come to a point in the middle of my hand. Over the dress I wear a sleeveless, black velvet overcoat that also falls to the floor. A gold band holds my hair out of my face, and the makeup lady will attach a fall to the back of my head and do it up in a complicated bun. I look nothing like myself in this getup. When I have it on, I feel one hundred percent like a queen and I'm starting to understand why Lady Macbeth wanted it so bad. In this costume I walk the stage with perfect posture and hold my head high, like Scottish royalty.

Simon's costume is very simple: brown pants with knee-high brown leather boots, a loose white shirt with a metallic mesh vest over top, and a big leather belt with a place for his sword. He looks very dashing in it. It's hard to believe that we're just over two weeks away from opening night. Even though I feel ready, I get a bit queasy when I try to imagine it.

After rehearsal, I skip the diner and go right home. My mom has a plate of sugar cookies in the shape of bats on the kitchen table, and I take a few with me when I go across the street to see Patience. Her mom shows me to her bedroom, which resembles a crime scene. If you didn't know Patience, you would call the police and report a robbery. It looks as if someone was searching for hidden money and ransacked the place. I think the walls used to be white but it's hard to tell. Patience has crayoned a mural that covers every bit of wall space she can reach. For now, though, she's out of commission. She's lying in her airplane bed with her leg propped up on a stack of pillows and she's reading a picture book that she puts down as soon as she sees me.

"Clare! Hurray! Will you paint my toenails?" She thrusts a bottle of black nail polish at me.

"Sure," I say, looking around for a chair. I wade through the dolls, books, Lego, plastic animals and cars and grab a pink plastic Barbie chair. I put it next to Patience's bed and squeeze myself into it. My knees are at shoulder level.

"Here." I hand her the bag of cookies.

She peers inside. "Mom! Bring milk! We've got cookies here!"

Her mom shows up a minute later carrying a plastic cup of milk with a bendy straw in it. She asks me if I'd like anything but I tell her I can't stay too long. Patience looks upset to hear this.

"Stay for supper! We're having ravioli. I'll eat off a tray with Winnie the Pooh on it and you can have Sleeping Beauty!"

"Thanks, but I can't."

Patience's mom leaves us alone, and Patience sips her milk and eats a bat cookie in between asking me questions. I get to work on her toenails.

"Do you know that it's Halloween in three days?"

"Yes, I do."

"I can't go trick-or-treating because I got run over." She blows bubbles into her milk.

"I know. That's too bad. What were you going to be?"

"A fireman or a ballerina but it doesn't matter anymore. I have to stay in bed like a baby."

"But you're not a baby, you're a brave girl. Did you know that?"

"Yup. The nurse at the hospital told me. His name is Jeff and he has a dog named Sadie."

"I have a dog, too, remember?" I ask.

"Can he come over?"

"My dog is a she. Her name is Elsie. I'll bring her next time."

"That would be nice." She sighs dramatically.

I chat with Patience and blow on her toenails until her mom comes in and tells her it's time for a pain pill. I say goodbye and Patience asks if she can hug me. I lean over her bed and she wraps her sticky hands around my neck and squeezes. She whispers into my ear loud enough for anyone in the house and probably the neighbourhood to hear. "Come back later and get me out of here. They're trying to kill me."

I unstick myself from Patience and smile at her mom, who pretends not to have heard.

"So, I'll see you tomorrow." I wink at her.

She winks back at me. "Right. See you tomorrow."

As I walk out her bedroom door behind her mom, Patience says in the same hoarse whisper, "Bring a flash-light and a big knife."

I give her a thumbs-up.

I say goodbye to Patience's mom and cross the street to my house, stopping at the curb to look both ways first.

# Chapter 25

*"Eye of newt and toe of frog,*
*Wool of bat and tongue of dog."*
SECOND WITCH

Allison and I decide to be murdered cheerleaders for Halloween. We hit the thrift store after school the day before and come up with two skirts and two gold sweaters. Our outfits set us back four dollars each. My mom hems the skirts and sews the letter "D" (for Dead) on the front of each sweater. Allison and I make blue and gold pompoms out of crepe paper.

On Halloween night, Aunt Rusty comes over to help us with the makeup because she has a lot of experience with looking like a dead person. Allison cuts the handle off a plastic knife, glues it to her sweater and surrounds it with fake blood. I have a fake bullet hole that I stick to my forehead. Aunt Rusty puts greyish-yellow makeup on our faces and darkens our eyes. We stuff our bras with tissues (lots of them) and put our hair in high ponytails (Allison's is real, mine's fake). The finishing touch is a purplish-blue lipstick. The effect is fabulous. My mom gets out her camera and we pose slumped over on the sofa with our eyes closed.

The party is for the cast and crew of *Macbeth* and all their friends. It's at a small community hall that Eric gets to use because he lives in the neighbourhood. Before we leave for the party we run across the street and scare the pants off Patience, who giggles with delight when she realizes that it's us. She tries to trick us into staying by telling us that her parents are torturing her, but we don't buy it. We leave her some candy and make a hasty retreat. Aunt Rusty drops us at the hall on her way to her own Halloween bash. She's going as an oracle. I'm not sure what that looks like.

Outside the hall we can hear "The Monster Mash" playing on the stereo. We go inside and say hello to Eric, who's dressed as an alien doctor, and his wife, who's dressed as a vampire nurse. Allison wasn't expecting Troy to be there but he is (I think it's pretty obvious that he's stalking her). He looks great in a pinstriped gangster suit with a plastic machine gun and a black fedora hat. Allison and I head over to the punch bowl for some Piña Ghoulada punch served up by Quasimodo. We stand on the sidelines, sipping our punch, and watch the crowd dance. This is the first Halloween party I've ever been to. Every other year I've stayed home and given out candy to a thousand screaming kids in Wal-Mart costumes. The costumes tonight are so good that it's hard to tell who's who.

Troy waits exactly five minutes before he asks Allison to dance. She hands me her pompoms and punch to hold. I pour her punch into mine and stand there alone. Simon and Sylvia walk in together dressed as Boris and Natasha. I dive for the girls' bathroom because I don't want Simon to see me standing there like a loser, holding two sets of pompoms. I fix my ponytail and touch up my lipstick with a tube I'm storing in my huge bra. When I come out, Eric grabs me and pulls me onto the dance floor. He takes a set of pompoms from me and performs a complicated cheerleading routine. His wife takes photos from the sidelines. Simon and Sylvia are dancing together, and when Simon sees me he laughs at my costume. He bumps into a dancing banana and excuses himself. Sylvia and Simon dance like an old married couple. I try not to watch them. They're having way too much fun.

A parent dressed as a pirate comes in the door carrying a stack of pizzas, and the dance floor empties as everyone heads for the food. Allison and I wait in line for the vegetarian pizza and then sit at one of the little tables. Simon and Sylvia join us seconds later. Troy is close behind, and he grabs a chair and squeezes between Allison and Sylvia. Simon asks me how Patience is doing and I fill him in. It seems as if he really cares. I'm feeling very uncomfortable sitting there talking to Simon with Sylvia watching, but she's not actually watching; she's talking to Allison and Troy. I don't think she would even care if Simon planted another kiss on me right now. In her eyes I'm probably the least threatening girl in the whole school, even dressed as a busty cheerleader. I know that she's probably the only girl for Simon and that they'll probably get married one day and have seven kids, but I like to think that maybe there's a tiny part of Simon she doesn't know. Simon is the type of person who can look into your eyes and catch a glimpse of your soul. I understand that because I see it every time he looks at me. Maybe that's all I get. Maybe I should be satisfied with that.

After we finish our pizza, "The Time Warp" comes on the stereo and Simon pulls me onto the dance floor. Dancing with Simon is more of a spectator sport, which is okay with me because I'm a terrible dancer. He's got some great moves and he doesn't care who's watching. I love that about him.

Allison and I slip out of the party at five minutes to ten and wait on the curb for my mom, who's coming to pick us up at ten because it's a school night. We practise our cheerleading on the sidewalk in front of the hall. Right when we're in the middle of another stupid routine, a little Volkswagen bug drives past us really slowly. The four people in the car are all clowns. We wave our pompoms at them and they wave back. The Volkswagen pulls up to the stop sign on the corner and stops. All the clowns get out and run around the car backward, honking their horns and tripping over their big feet. One of them is a girl. Even under all that makeup, I know who she is. It's Elsa. We watch them get back in the bug and drive away.

I look at Allison. "Did you see what I saw?"

She nods. "You never know what you'll see on Halloween night."

My mom arrives right on time, and we drop Allison off at her house. The streets are dark and empty now except for the odd adult in costume coming home from a party. We pass a witch and a Cat in the Hat walking up the side-walk together. I love grown-up Halloween.

At home, Elsie barks at me till she gets a good sniff and realizes who it is. I go upstairs and take one more look at myself as a cheerleader before I pull the bullet hole off my forehead and get in the shower. The washcloth turns greyish-purple as I wipe all the makeup off. One murdered cheerleader down the drain.

I get into bed and think about Simon and Sylvia, who were still on the dance floor when we left. I imagine their romantic goodbye when he leaves her and goes off into the night, but then I wonder how romantic all that kissing can be when it happens all the time, when you don't have to yearn for it and dream about it. Is it all downhill after the first kiss or does it keep getting better? I kiss Elsie on the forehead and she puts her paw over my mouth. It smells like butterscotch.

# Chapter 26

Al Pacino and Sean Penn walk across the stage to the podium wearing black tuxedos. They read the nominees for best actress.

"Meryl Streep in *Till Tomorrow*," reads Al. The audience cheers.

"Winona Ryder in *Dream Girl*," reads Sean. The audience goes nuts.

"Natalie Portman in *Daylight*," reads Al. The audience cheers.

"And Clare Ferron in *A Gypsy Flees*," reads Sean. The audience roars.

Al tears open the envelope. He looks at us over his reading glasses. "And the Academy Award goes to Clare Ferron for *A Gypsy Flees*." The audience is on its feet. I stand up and start out for the stage wearing my underwear with the little red hearts and a grey T-shirt with Mighty Mouse on the front. I climb the steps to the stage in my bare feet. Sean and Al are grinning at me from the top of the stairs, and the gold statuette sparkles in Sean's hands, but every time I get close to them, more stairs appear. I start taking the stairs two at a time but new stairs appear twice as fast. The audience's cheers turn into jeers and boos and Al and Sean walk offstage with my statuette, shaking their heads. I try to call to them but my voice won't work.

I wake up with the bedsheets tangled around my legs, and my Mighty Mouse T-shirt twisted into a ball. I look at the clock. It's 7:00 a.m.

Twelve hours till opening night. No more rehearsals. No more fittings. No more working on this and fixing that and trying this a different way. I couldn't be better prepared and I couldn't be more terrified. I don't want to go to school today. In fact, I don't ever want to go to school again. I want to devote my life to acting. School seems pointless.

The snow has politely held off, but it feels moments away as I walk briskly to the corner where I meet Allison. The frosty air is freezing my nose hairs. Allison is right on time because we talk the minute before we leave the house and our watches are synchronized.

"Hi. It's cold, it's cold, it's cold!" says Allison, puffs of vapour escaping as she speaks.

"I know. Hurry, my lungs are freezing, my feet are numb, my nose is frostbitten."

"Okay! We're not on an arctic expedition. It's not even snowing yet."

We walk quickly, jumping up and down at the corners, waiting for the light to change. Once the school is in sight we relax a little, knowing we'll be warm soon. We pass the sign out in front of the school that advertises the play. A banner has been added that says OPENING NIGHT. As if I need to be reminded. My stomach does a flip-flop. The play is sold out tonight, mostly because all the cast's families and friends go the first night, but Eric says ticket sales are brisk and most of our costs have been covered already. We'll make up the rest in pop sales at intermission.

A big black suv passes us and pulls up in front of the school. Ginny jumps out all warm and rosy-cheeked, minus the scarves, hats and mittens Allison and I are wearing. She dashes up the walk and in the front door of the school like a girl without a care in the world.

At my locker I blow on my hands, trying to warm them up so I can work the combination on my lock. Down the hall, Allison is doing the same. Ginny is busy at her locker, too. She's made a new friend, a pretty eighth grader named Morgan. Ginny seems to be briefing her on what the job of being Ginny's friend entails. Morgan looks delighted and more than ready to take on the position. Darla is nowhere to be seen. I guess that's the thing about girls like Ginny. No matter what happens, they always seem to come out of it okay. When you're the most popular girl in eighth grade, it takes more than a minor scandal to get you down. That's the difference between Shakespeare and real life: Lady Macbeth goes insane and kills herself; Ginny regroups. Even the girls who know that Ginny stole and lied will probably come around. That's just the way it works in the brutally unfair world of junior high.

On the way to Math class I peek in at the theatre for a look at the stage. The carpenters are putting the finishing touches to it. It looks dark and old and musty. Eric and his clipboard are rushing about, but he still has that patented

"Eric Calm" in his eyes. When he sees me, he motions for me to come in because there's too much hammering to hear. We stand together and look at the stage.

"It looks great," I say.

"It does. It looks better than I ever dreamed it would. Are you ready?"

"Ready as I'll ever be." I gulp.

"Don't worry, I know you. You're going to ace it."

"You think so?"

"If I didn't, you wouldn't be my leading lady."

I blush and get out of the way of the students who are setting up rows of chairs.

I rush home after school for a quick dinner. My mom has opening-night jitters, too. She feeds me a bowl of home-made chicken soup and paces the kitchen while I eat, inventing little tasks like wiping up invisible crumbs and spots. It would be easier for her if she had a specific job, but all she has to do is get me there. I shower and pull my jeans on and she drives me back to school. She and my dad will come back in two hours.

Backstage, the makeup lady finishes the three witches' faces while the wardrobe manager helps them with their dresses. I'm right after them. I practise my lines while I'm waiting. Simon isn't there yet because he's a lot easier to put together.

The makeup lady puts my hair up. She attaches the fall to the back and pins it up. It looks like I have super-long hair. Then she pins the gold band into place and starts on my makeup. The wardrobe manager appears with my dress, which they carefully place over my head and zip up. I am *so* Lady Macbeth. They put a black choker with a large medallion on it around my neck and give me my rings — large, garish, fake rubies for each hand. Just as I'm taking a look in the mirror, Simon comes in, having narrowly missed seeing me in my underwear.

"Wow," he says, taking in the complete Lady Macbeth. "You look beautiful. I'm really glad I married you."

"Hello, my spineless husband," I tease.

Almost the whole cast is dressed now, and we look like a proper bunch of Scottish nobility with lots of servants and three witches. Astrid, my understudy, is standing by in case I pass out from nerves. Eric gathers us together for a little pep talk. He reminds us that the lights make it impossible to see the audience so we should act like it's not even there, while remembering to project. He also reminds us that we were able to pull this whole thing off in dress rehearsal so tonight should be a breeze. Easy for him to say. As soon as he's done we go back to the pre-play chaos.

From backstage we can hear the rustling of programs and murmurs from the front of the house as the audience take its seats. I suppress the urge to run out into the cold and away from all this pressure. After being invisible to these people for so many years, tonight I will dominate their lives for almost two hours. The thought makes me a little queasy.

On Eric's cue the soundman starts the music that will play for a few minutes until the opening music starts. (Eric has chosen "Golden Years" by David Bowie for the opening song, a modern take on an old theme.) Then we begin.

# Chapter 27

Scene 5 begins. I am standing alone onstage, reading aloud a letter from my husband, so I have a moment to collect myself and get comfortable with the idea of being out there. I hope the audience can't see that the letter I'm holding is shaking. (Waiting in the wings for four scenes, I suddenly developed a major case of flop sweat and the wardrobe manager had to take a hair dryer to my armpits. She did her best and told me to avoid lifting my arms too high.) When I finish the letter I gaze out into the darkness and continue:

> *"Glamis thou art, and Cawdor, and shalt be*
> *What thou art promised. Yet do I fear thy nature;*
> *It is too full o' th' milk of human kindness*
> *To catch the nearest way. Thou wouldst be great,*
> *Art not without ambition, but without*
> *The illness should attend it. What thou wouldst highly ..."*

Eric once told me that the trick to performing Shakespeare is to let the words flow like a song or a poem. Shakespeare wrote his plays in something called iambic pentameter, and it sounds like the beating of your heart: DaDUM, daDUM, daDUM. Eric says that if you think about that while you recite your lines, it can be very calming. It works. I take my time, careful not to rush my lines. I speak clearly and confidently. When Simon joins me on the stage I feel even more confident. He makes it look so easy. This spot on this stage is the place I want to be forever. I feel powerful and strong and beautiful and I never want it to end.

The audience is absolutely quiet. They're either loving it or they've left. Each scene flows into the next with only a tiny error here and there, nothing the audience could even notice. Before I know it, Act 3 is over and we're in intermission.

Makeup touches me up and wardrobe brings me my next costume, a multi-layered, cream-coloured dressing gown made of silk. Someone brings me a glass of water. I have a break because I'm not on again till Act 5. I watch with Simon from the wings as the witches begin Act 4. He squeezes my hand and then strides onstage. I understand why Simon didn't hesitate that day at the diner when I asked him what he wanted to be. He was born to act. When he's onstage the energy seems magically elevated. He told me that the fact that he can't see too much really helps. He refuses to wear his glasses because they don't fit the Macbeth image.

He addresses the witches:

> *"How now, you secret, black, and midnight hags?*
> *What is 't you do?"*

I wait in the wings, looking forward to my next scene.

I'm dying to be back onstage. My scene finally arrives.
It's the one I froze on two weeks ago. I try to wash the
imaginary blood from my hands.

> "... *Here's the smell of the blood still.*
> *All the perfumes of Arabia*
> *will not sweeten this little hand. O, O, O!*"

Things go along smoothly until, unfortunately, in the
very last scene, Macduff accidentally drops Macbeth's
bloodied head and it almost rolls off the stage before he
recovers it. Eric moans backstage. Macduff makes a good
save and actually makes it look like it was supposed to
happen that way. The music starts and the play is over.

The house lights go up and the cast comes together on
stage. We all bow at once. The audience is on its feet.
Simon and I step forward, holding hands, and bow again.
Aunt Rusty is in the fourth row, cheering enthusiastically.
Mr. Bianchini is standing next to her. Allison and Troy are
standing next to them with Allison's parents. My dad is
one row ahead of them, videotaping us. It must have driv-
en him crazy that videotaping was not allowed during the
performance. My mom is beaming and clapping, looking
as relieved as I feel that we pulled it off. In the back, wearing an elegant, wide-brimmed felt hat and a very smart
navy suit, is Elsa, smiling and blowing me a kiss.

Eric comes out from backstage and squeezes between
Simon and me and we all bow together. The crowd stays

on its feet. Opening night is somehow over. Relief washes over the cast and crew and we're giddy with excitement. We ham it up for photos and laugh and hug each other. My parents wait for me but I tell them to go ahead without me because we're all going out for coffee at "Café Dirt," which is what we renamed the diner. I invite Allison and Troy to come along, but Troy says he's tired, which really means that he wants to be alone with Allison, even if it's just for a few minutes.

We take off our makeup and hang up our costumes and head out into the cold night. While we were inside a light snow started to fall, and it coats the sidewalks and swirls around us as we make our way to the diner. It's sad to think that this might be one of the last times we gather there. I wouldn't miss it for the world.

## Chapter 28

It's too cold to sit out on the roof. Big flakes of snow are dancing outside my window, turning the roof to marshmallow. I lounge on my bed with a cup of hot chocolate and two unopened packs of photos fresh from the one-hour-photo place. I don't think there's anything quite as exciting as a pack of new photos. I tear the tape off the first pack and slide the photos out. Elsa appears and squeezes between Elsie and me, shoving Elsie's cold nose out of the way.

"Move it, furball!" She looks over my shoulder at the first photo of me in my Lady Macbeth costume. She sighs. "You looked so beautiful that night. I can't believe you had to go and kill yourself."

"Well, it is a tragedy."

"Yeah, about that? I vote for a comedy next year. Does Lady Macbeth get a say? No more tragedies, they're too depressing."

"Not only do I not get a say, I have to start from scratch and audition all over again."

"Ah, stop with the false modesty, you're a shoo-in."

I don't want to jinx anything, so I don't mention that Eric told me he wants me to audition for an exclusive drama camp next summer. Simon will be auditioning for the very same camp.

I flip through some photos of the cast onstage and suddenly stop at a photo taken after the play. Simon and I are standing together. His arm is around my shoulders and I'm looking up at him and smiling like a beauty pageant contestant.

"Now there's a handsome couple," says Elsa. "What's the plan? When's he ditching the girlfriend?"

"He's not."

"That's a shame." She scratches Elsie behind the ears. "Right, dog breath?"

My mom took a photo of Aunt Rusty and Mr. Bianchini, who are looking very much like a couple, standing next to each other with their fingertips touching. Mr. Bianchini is smiling the crooked smile I fell in love with a thousand years ago.

The next photo is Troy and Allison mugging for the camera. Elsa and I stare at it for a minute. The photo after it is exactly the same except they're both smiling pleasantly, and I know my mom must have told them that she would keep going until she got a good one. I've been there.

My favourite photo in the pack is one of Allison and me. We didn't know that my mom was taking it. I'm still in my costume and Allison is leaning in, looking at my necklace. I'm laughing and we look like we've been friends forever.

"She really likes you. I think you've got yourself a soul-mate there."

I smile at Elsa. "You think so?"

"Well, she'll never be me. Don't forget, I had a hand in raising you."

"Thanks for that."

When I tear open the second pack of photos to show Elsa our Halloween costumes, she's gone. I watch the snow swirl outside and place my hand on the cold glass windowpane. "Thank you," I whisper.

Later that day I pull the box that holds my comic book collection out of my closet. I haven't looked at it in weeks. I open the box and lovingly flip through them, pulling out my favourites and filing them back in. I close the box and carry it across the street.

Patience's mom lets me in. Patience is sleeping, one of those rare moments when she's not moving. Her tangled orange hair is splayed across the pillow and she's snoring a little. I sit in the pink Barbie chair for a few minutes watching her. Then I put the box of comic books next to her bed and walk back across the street to my house.

Christmas Eve at the mall is the height of desperation. Basically, it's a big game of musical chairs, except the chairs are gifts and when the Christmas music stops, whoever doesn't have a gift is the loser. Most of the people in line to have their gifts wrapped are suburban dads with the unmistakeable look of fear in their eyes. Allison knows she has them over a barrel and she's using it to her advantage.

"This is a really beautiful necklace," she smiles. "I'm sure your wife will love it and she'll also be pleased to know that all contributions are helping in the fight against breast cancer."

The man drops a couple of dollars into the collection jar.

"It's a very big fight, sir," says Allison. The man empties his wallet into the jar. Satisfied, she hands him a pink ribbon. "For your wife," she says, smiling.

While we wrap, I ask her about her trip to the science

museum with Paul. She looks all dreamy like someone who just went on a date with Johnny Depp or something.

"Paul and I connect on a million different levels," she says, all starry-eyed.

A million different levels? One level or maybe half a level, but a million? I just don't get it. Paul, by the way, hasn't called me once since he's been back. I mean, sure, we don't connect on a million different levels or anything like that but we have known each other for a really long time and a phone call might be nice. I haven't had my usual hour-long daily phone chats with Allison either now that Paul's arrived on the scene. Yes, I do realize that she's standing right next to me as I'm thinking this but those phone chats are really important to me.

I'm waiting for Allison to ask me how the band practice thing at Vince's went but it never happens, so I just tell her. She gets a strange look on her face.

"What's that look?" I ask.

"What look?"

"That look you just gave me. You know the one."

She looks down. "Well, it's just that Simon called to invite me to his sledding party on Saturday night and, um, don't take this the wrong way, but he doesn't think that Vince is the kind of guy you should be hanging around with."

"Sheesh, when did Simon become the leading authority on suitable dating partners? And how is this any of his business? You're all acting like Vince is a convicted felon or something!"

"Don't get mad at me. I don't even know the guy. I'm just telling you what I heard because you're my friend and I care about you."

I look over at Vince as he crouches down to talk to a little girl in line to see Santa. He brushes a strand of hair out of his eyes. My pulse quickens and my stomach does a little somersault. It seems to me that the more people tell me he's bad for me, the more attracted I am to him. What's that all about? ...

... I'm really wishing Elsa were here to put things in perspective for me. I put my head down on my pillow and watch Maude swim lazily around the Eiffel Tower in her glass bowl.

Dear Elsa,

It's Christmas Eve and I'm missing you terribly. Remember that guy I told you about? The elf named Vince? Well, I really like him a lot (A LOT) but everyone seems to think I should stay away from him. I'm still going to that party on Saturday night. I'm a little nervous about it. What should I wear? How should I act?

... I really hope you aren't lonely. I hope you're with friends. I miss you.

Merry Christmas,

Clare

# Double-Dare Clare

978-1-55192-983-5
$10.95 CDN / $9.95 US

Ask your bookseller about
*Double-Dare Clare*
and other great titles
from Raincoast Books!

## THE CLARE SERIES IS ANCIENT-FOREST FRIENDLY

By printing *Not Fair, Clare* on paper made from 100% recycled fibre rather than virgin tree fibre, Raincoast Books has made the following ecological savings:

- 21 trees
- 2,011 kilograms of carbon dioxide (equivalent to driving an average North American car for about five months)
- 17 million BTUs (equivalent to the power consumption of a North American home for over two months)
- 12,322 litres of water
- 753 kilograms of solid waste diverted from landfill

Environmental savings were estimated by Markets Initiative using the Environmental Defense Paper Calculator. For more information, visit www.papercalculator.org.

**RAINCOAST BOOKS**
*www.raincoast.com*

ANCIENT FOREST
**FRIENDLY**

## About the Author

Yvonne Prinz was born and raised in Edmonton, Alberta. *Not Fair, Clare* is her second novel in a series of books about the quirky and loveable Clare and her savvy alter ego, Elsa. Book One in the series, *Still There, Clare*, was first published by Raincoast Books in 2004. Yvonne lives in the San Francisco Bay area, where she and her husband founded a chain of independent record stores.

*www.stillthereclare.com*